WED

KARC

(A novel based on true incidents)

ANIL KUMAR GUPTA

RAINBOW
PUBLISHERS

ISBN: 978-81-9094-410-6

Published by
Rainbow Publishers
Noida, India
www.rainbowpublishers.in

Author
E.mail: author@anilkumargupta.net
Web site: www.anilkumargupta.net

Typeset in 12/14.5 Adobe Calson Pro
SwaRadha Typesetting

Printed at: Fortune India Printer, Noida

Dedicated to all parents

ACKNOWLEDGEMENTS

To say this is my novel would be totally untrue. It is based on experiences of wonderful parents and children who shared it with me and it is their expectations, dreams and occurrences which are in the form of this book in your hand.

To start with I'd like to acknowledge the help I got from all the parents, whose rich experiences of going through the marriage match-making process for their children helped me in writing this book.

'Wedding Aaj Kal-Karolbagh to Kerala' has been an interesting and enlightening project, brought to fruition through the efforts of my family members.

I thank my wife Neetu, who provided me good ideas and deeper insight into the changing wedding customs and trends all around. She encouraged me to complete it in a short time. She read my manuscript and offered great suggestions.

As always, my sons Prateek, Pravir and daughter-in-law Himani kept my writing spirits high.

I express my thanks to my son Aniket aged eight years, encouraging me by expressing funny ideas and relaxing me with his constant banter. He suggested the title of this book.

I thank all my colleagues, friends and well wishers who knew I was writing a book and provided their encouragement.

Lastly, I would like to thank the cities of Delhi and Kochi and its people who I always had in my mind while writing this book.

Comments for my first novel
"The Journey is the Reward"

".....I whole heartedly agree with the thesis of your book that happiness lies in the way and not at the end of the journey."

Dr Shashi Tharoor, the noted international writer, novelist and India's Minister of State for External Affairs.

...His quest for drawing a parallel line between religion and Science inspired him to write his first novel......... Anil is deeply fascinated by the similarities amongst different religions.....

Editors, http://www.BureaucracyToday.Com
5th August

...The novel is about a person who is finding answers to question bothering us in our daily lives. The main character considers himself as a gift of God. The questions are simple but the answers are complex and philosophical. On the whole, an attempt has been made to satisfy the curiosity of readers who want answers to their queries...

(Translated from Dainik Jagran Lucknow, Column-Book Watch, 10th, July,2009)

...."In this novel, the author has answered questions boggling the mind of society....'

(Hindustan (Newspaper), Noida, 8/7/2009

"...changes in human body and mind have been tested scientifically in this book......"

Punjab Kesari (Newspaper), 8/7/2009

"......It reminded me of the book "The Monk who sold his Ferari...... ...keenly looking forward to see many more...

Rakesh Garg, Executive Director, FCI,
New Delhi, India

On my last visit to India, I bought this book The Journey is the Reward, from airport book shop. The author has handled the subject very well. May be he should have elaborated a bit more towards the end of the book. The concepts explained are revolutionary in character. A must read for every one interested in the subject.-

Richard Bates, Wellington, New Zealand

...Congratulations. It is an honor to the whole service, especially UP cadre. All the very best...

Prabhat Kumar, IAS

...Having bought the book from CP Delhi, I went through it chapter by chapter. The last few chapters are really enlightening. I congratulate the author for the painstaking study of the subject.

Gizenzy, Milan, Italy

ONE

For Sunil Chawla the morning of 22nd June was unlike any other. He was the first to wake up today and walked towards the grille window and looked out. The rain had stopped, but a pale mist hung in the air. The earth was awakening, its fertility rejuvenated. It smelt of mud and grass, fresh and new. The night had ended and the sun was beginning to peek over the horizon, heralding a brand-new day. He picked up the *Sunday Hindustan Times*. Hurriedly, he flipped through the classified advertisement pages searching until he found the matrimonial advertisement he had placed for his son Anil.

'*Looking for suitable bride for Delhi-based Punjabi, handsome, 26, 5' 11", fair, non-manglic boy, working for Multinational IT company in Noida. Salary 20 Lakhs p.a. Father highly respected businessman and brother well settled. Business families from Delhi and Punjab preferred.*'

Sunil Chawla smiled with satisfaction, as if he has seen his name and number in the list of 'elGordo' Spanish lottery winners.

Popularly known as Chawla Bhai, Sunil was every inch a Delhite, born in Chawri Bazaar to refugee parents who had migrated from the West Pakistan. Chawla Bhai's father had owned a saree shop in Chandni Chowk and did not believe in the virtues of higher education so he involved his entire family in the family business starting from scratch but raising his family of three sons and two daughters reasonably well. Only five years after coming to Delhi he fulfilled his dreams of owning a house in Parathe-wali Gali. Until his death in 2003 he had been the head of the Chandni Chowk Merchants Association.

Chawla Bhai had learnt to count money before he learnt the alphabet. He and his brothers had quickly expanded the family business by opening two more saree shops in the relatively modern neighborhoods of Model town and Karolbagh. Being the eldest, he preferred to manage the ancestral Chandni Chowk saree shop. His younger brothers, Pramod and Ramesh, managed the Model Town and Karol Bagh shops but continued to live in the same house as Sunil till both got married to girls from business families of Karolbagh.

Sunil Chawla's wife Ritu, also from Delhi, belonged to a family that owned two restaurants in South Delhi. Her father, Balvinder Ahuja had owned a small eatery outlet in Daryaganj thirty years back. A social climber of sorts, he'd provided good education to his daughters. He never failed to brag about his daughter being the only University graduate in the neighborhood. Balvinder liked Sunil Chawla and his family and agreed for a matrimonial alliance.

Ritu was tall and beautiful. She had graduated from Delhi University and had several friends in the Delhi social circuit. An avid shopper and member of many prestigious clubs, she devoted her time and energy to her two sons until her youngest son Anil went to the United States for a master's degree in IT. With her children grown up, Ritu looked for excitement in her friends and social clubs. Her eldest son Amit's wife looked after household affairs.

Chawla Bhai felt happy providing Ritu with every comfort. He loved her dearly (more so when he was drunk) and called her titlee or butterfly in private moments. She wasn't sure what he meant by the endearment. She was indeed a butterfly flitting from one social party to another. On their silver wedding anniversary her husband had gifted to her Honda Accord. On every social occasion she looked for faux 'designer' clothes in Karol Bagh market because she couldn't afford the real ones every day.

Ritu considered her eldest son Amit's wife, Lovely naïve and lacking in social graces. Lovely belonged to a rich family of Punjabi transporters in the Azad Market and her rich family's background stopped her mother-in-law from running her down before others. Considering discretion to be the better part of valor, Ritu motivated Lovely to join swimming and dancing classes. Her voice was harsh and grating. With practice it was made mellow and refined. She seemed artless and callow. Through imitation she became urbane and genteel. Since Lovely had not her University education, Ritu hired the same English tutor who had taught her to help Lovely brush up on her English accent and vocabulary. Ritu started Lovely's transformation with a haircut, snipping away at her long black tresses, giving what the Anglo-Indian hairstylist called 'an easy shoulder-length flippy brunette hairstyle.'

When Ritu became confident that her daughter-in-law was ready to move socially, she started taking her out to parties and club-meetings and presented her as a graduate from University of London. Lovely had devotedly learnt the university's address and the courses it offered. The rest, she managed to concoct without feeling embarrassed.

The Chawla family doted on Anil, the only family member to go out to US and achieve something. As he now had a cushy job in an international Company, Global Logix in Noida bordering Delhi, everyone was concerned about his marriage. Ritu loved having parents of girls enquire about her son but neither she nor Sunil Chawla considered any girl on earth to be good enough match for Anil. Their unbridled adulation and ridiculous boasting embarrassed Anil. As both Chawla Bhai and his eldest son Amit were busy either working in the shop or drinking late at the club, Ritu and Lovely had taken the search and selection of a suitable girl for Anil upon themselves.

They had asked Chawla Bhai to put a matrimonial ad in the news-paper and the whole family (except Anil) was eagerly awaiting the results.

***

TWO

Adinath G. Ramchandran Nair returned from his morning walk, opened the gate and walked in; a pesky little dog appeared on the lawn and proceeded to water the flowers. Then it shut its eyes and relived itself right there in the center of the green carpet of grass. Nair didn't dislike dogs but was annoyed by the blissful look on its face as it closed its eyes and let go in four equal instalments.

He heard Mrs. Bhasin, the fat lady call from the balcony of the flat on the first floor, 'Baby, come back right now. Your mamma wants you. Don't make her angry baccha.'

Nair climbed upstairs, but didn't want to pick up a fight so early in the morning. He wanted to discuss the matter with Mrs. Bhasin amiably. But the dog squinting at him and wagging its tail furiously against the curtain annoyed him further and he told her in no uncertain terms to keep her baccha strapped.

Nair became sure it wasn't going to be a good day for him. The north Indian Mrs. Bhasin and her dog had spoiled his mood once again and this time very early in the morning. Nair wondered how callous the north Indians could be about their neighbors.

Nair turned on his laptop while his wife Lathika Devi sat beside him and logged on to his favorite website, www.Keralamatrimony.com. Their inbox showed five new messages. After both of them had read the messages, Nair deleted all of them.

'It's difficult to find good boys these days,' Lathika said, frustrated.

'What's the hurry? Parvathi is just twenty five'.

'I shall feel at ease only after she's married. She's working for several months now. I don't like girls being single and working for long.'

'I trust our Parvathi,' Nair said. 'She did well in the US and her name never got linked up with any boy there. She's different from other girls.'

Nair was working as a Director in the Ministry of Health, Government of India. For the last thirty years he lived in Delhi, very far from his native city Kochi in Kerala. He had joined the Central Secretariat Service long before and had remained in Delhi while his wife taught Psychology in Saraswati College. Their combined salary plus the rental income from property in Kochi was sufficient to maintain a comfortable lifestyle in Delhi. They had only one child, Parvathi.

Nair and Lathika married twenty-six years earlier. Lathika who had come from Trivandrum, was visiting Kochi for the first time. She met Nair on the Loafer's Street in Fort Kochi and they were attracted to each other. The two families matched the young people's horoscopes and eventually the couple exchanged rings. Neither family intended the wedding to be a big affair. After a visit to the temple of Lord Ayappa, they were married in a neighboring *kalayana mandappam* or marriage hall. A year later Parvathi was born.

Parvathi after doing Masters in Science from UC Berkeley had now joined a software multinational company, Global Logix, in Noida. She was beautiful, fair, extrovert and familiar with Delhi life and culture since she grew up there. She had left for US after doing her Bachelors from Indian Institute of Technology, Delhi despite her mother's reluctance to send her abroad. Lathika always wished that her daughter should either join her best friend Rekha's Fashion Designing Institute or take up a job in Gurgaon. Nair wanted Parvathi to go to Gulf where he had several relatives and because she had already been offered a lucrative job through campus placement in IIT. But Parvathi stood firm and chose to do Masters from US. After weeks of serious discussions, Nair and Lathika agreed on one condition-after her return, she will marry a Kerala boy chosen by her parents.

When she joined Global Logix, most of her male colleagues, young and old were attracted towards her while some were overawed by her accomplishments. As her face resembled a Bollywood leading actress, Vidya Balan, a race started among the eligible bachelors to come close to her and between the female co-workers to hate her. Before the race could pick enough momentum, it seemed to be over as she was seen spending most of her time with her colleague, Anil.

Anil Chawla, the Chief Supervisor was considered the probable choice for Parvathi's affections. He was a tall, slim and muscular young man who had done Masters from an American University. Anil was flamboyant, had the latest gizmos, drove a Mercedes given by his father on his return to India and had a clever head on his shoulders. During his last one and half years in the Company several girls yearning for his affections threw themselves upon him but their overtures could not progress beyond short flings and one-night stands. Shiela Arora was the only girl with whom his friendship lasted for some time until it ended abruptly as Parvathi appeared all of a sudden and captured Anil's heart and mind. Sheila could never forgive Parvathi for being a spoil-sport in her quest to entice and woo Anil, a rich, successful and handsome bachelor.

***

THREE

Anil went about the task of dating girls in Global Logix with a lot of planning. For example, he evaluated them on different parameters-looks, intellect, nature, outlook and education. Needless to say he would look for the very best in all these aspects; his expectations often exceeded the rational, thus causing disappointment.

Anil's first brush was with a pretty girl called Rakhee, two months after his return to India. She was quite a contrast to Anil. She was chirpy, fun-loving, uncomplicated, spontaneous and above all 'a natural'. She would laugh freely. They got along quite well for a while but shied away from being the first to propose. Both were perhaps strategically harping on the friendship plank, hoping that the other would tread the extra mile of making a formal proposal. This constant pregnant expectation of "you do it first" started getting on Anil's nerves. Somewhere, in his heart, he had made up his mind that Rakhee was not a wife material; instead she was just *time* pass. This categorization had to do with intellectual compatibility issue; he realized that chirpy, fun loving, spontaneous Rakhee would charm him, no doubt, but perhaps won't have the intellect to engage him in the kind of absorbing interactions he liked.

Strangely, Anil like many other males had come to categorize women in two broad categories: the time pass variety, the girlfriend sort, one he could date and have fun with; and the other, the wife material, in whom he saw the virtues of being mother of his children. Rakhee, by his perception, belonged to the former. However girls being girls, Rakhee was taken in by the good natured flirting of Anil and instinctively got closer to him. But, Anil, like most men might have, interpreted this friendliness as a gesture of the girl wanting something 'more'. Anil was encouraged by Rajesh and made a pass at her.... And that was the end of their friendship.

'Bloody hell!' He cursed, 'why do these women suddenly start behaving like prudes?' Anil had complained impulsively to Rajesh and Rakesh, his colleagues and friends, only to be reminded that unlike him, others have a right to be serious.

After his short time pass with Rakhee, Anil met a string of girls which led him to add another category – available for one night stands- to his existing categorization of time pass variety and wife material.

His short affair with Sheila was neither a *time* pass nor he considered her a wife material. She was beautiful, curvaceous, intelligent, and liberal and had a stable career in Global Logix. She had the guts to express her love openly. She used to hold Anil's hand and kiss him without feeling shy. But it was her ambitious nature which made her stand out. A keen observer and lover of luxury cars, she had dreams to make it big in US. Anil was only a stepping stone.

'With a bit of luck, one day you'll find me staying in the White House in Washington DC.' She had boastfully predicted her future to her friend.

Anil never felt sure of her, had unwittingly lowered his guards but their association couldn't progress beyond lunches, dinners and movies, this time Sheila using him to date and have fun with. It did not take him long to realize that she was not dependable and a wife material, as Sheila dumped him for someone more attractive to her. It was then he saw Parvathi and felt she was the girl he would like to settle down with.

Parvathi appeared different to Anil. She did not show off her past association with US, usually dressed in a saree and kept quiet unless spoken to. She avoided making eye contact with any one. She looked a marriage material which every man with lust in mind and a roving eye would like to settle down with or take home to meet his parents. She had a Hyundai Santro which she drove herself.

Anil, an experienced man in these matters, didn't take long to decide that Parvathi was *the* girl for him.

****

Anil was on the prowl, looking for every opportunity to talk to Parvathi. His charm and persistence soon yielded the desired results.

Outside office, everyone waited for the rain to stop so that they could walk to the car park. Anil came to Parvathi making his way through the crowd and said, 'We should have a covered car-parking here.'

Parvathi just nodded her head remaining silent.

'I learnt you are also April born like me?' Anil had gone through her profile on the company computer and tried to start a conversation.

'Yes I am.'

'And you were born in Delhi like me?'

'Yes I was.'

'You love to read fiction.'

'How do you know?' Parvathi was curious.

'Simple. I read the hobby section in your profile. In fact I also love reading novels. It transports me to the world of fantasy. Moreover I learn a lot from novels.'

'What are you reading these days?' Parvathi asked.

'*The Associate*' by John Grisham. It's about legal profession in US and the dilemma of a man who is blackmailed. I have read few pages.'

'I am reading an old one, Fasting Feasting, by Anita Desai. It's a good story.'

'About what?'

'Its about a spinster daughter of a close-knit Indian family who is trapped at home, smothered by her overbearing parents and their traditions and about her sister and brother. It's an interesting novel.'

'You like family dramas or social type novels?'

'Not exactly, I read all kind of fiction.'

'Great. What a pleasant surprise! We both are interested in novels. We have a lot to talk about. Let's have coffee at Radisson on our way back home,' Anil said. 'But we both have to drive our cars, I presume.' He asked.

'Yes I drive my own car. What about you?'

'Same here,' Anil said. 'The rain has stopped. Let's meet at Radisson coffee shop. I'll go first. You can follow me.' Anil stepped outside to drive his car as Parvathi followed.

Once inside the coffee shop, Anil and Parvathi ordered for Pastry and coffee.

'How long have you been working here?' asked Parvathi.

'I joined last year. Earlier I was in US for my Masters degree.'

'Really?' She asked. 'I was there too. In UC Berkley. Where were you?'

'I was in Carnegie Mellon, Pittsburgh,' Anil answered. 'It's great to know someone who studied in US.'

The conversation shifted and they told each other about their families. All of a sudden Parvathi realized that they had been talking for almost an hour and asked for the bill. Anil didn't allow her to pay, settled the bill, shook hands and walked out toward their cars.

Before starting his car Anil sent a SMS to Parvathi, 'Thanks. I enjoyed talking to you. I'll look forward to meet you again tomorrow.'

Beep…Beep. He got the reply. 'Thanks for coffee. I enjoyed talking to you.'

During the drive home, both Anil and Parvathi kept thinking about each other.

Next evening at 4 pm, Parvathi's mobile showed a new message waiting to be read. The message was from Anil suggesting coffee in Hyatt on their way back. Parvathi smiled as she received another SMS, a repeat of the earlier one. She sent her reply, 'See you there at six thirty.'

It became a regular feature to meet every evening for coffee at some restaurant but they chose a different restaurant every day during last one and half months. Gradually the conversation became more personal. Anil started complementing her on her dress and her looks. Parvathi used to sit right opposite Anil in the restaurant. She always looked beautiful in Indian wear.

She found him staring at her and asked, 'What are you staring at? Do I look different?'

'I am just admiring your ravishing suit, pink *kameez*, sky blue *pyjami* and a blended *chunni* with shiny stones making uneven lines on it, your long and silky hair and glossy lips. You look great in this north Indian dress.'

'Thank you,' she blushed.

'I wish everybody in this restaurant would vanish for a couple of hours so that I can keep staring at you.'

'Come on Anil. I can't be here for next two hours,' Parvathi said adjusting her *chunni* which kept sliding down her right shoulder.

As week days were no longer enough for their meetings, they decided to watch a movie next Sunday and dine out.

Anil picked her from South Extension market where Parvathi had parked her car. They went to watch a movie *Bachna Ae Haseeno*. There were few scenes which touched Parvathi and she unknowingly squeezed Anil's resting arm and he clutched her fingers tightly in his. Later, they dined at Hotel Intercontinental. They talked about the movie, the playboy kind of role of its main character and his ultimate success in finding his love.

'What's the craziest thing you've done in your life?' Anil asked abruptly.

'Hmm…. Let me think. Well, once I slipped out of my class right under my cock-eyed Professor's nose after he had taken the attendance.'

'That's not crazy'

'Yeah? What's your craziest deed then?'

'Well, I am going to do that now.'

Parvathi wondered what Anil was up to.

'I am going to ask you a difficult question.'

Parvathi looked at him clueless.

'Will you marry me?'

Parvathi wondered if she was hallucinating. The question kept ringing in her ears. She found herself in a very unusual situation. She had been proposed to in life for the first time, that too by an incredibly eligible bachelor. Her ecstasy made her feel nervous. Her nervousness made her procrastinate.

'Well, I don't really know what to say. I am flattered that of all girls you must be meeting regularly, you found interest in me. May I ask you what interested you about me so much?'

Anil thought.

'Well, let me see if I have an answer. I guess you appear very pristine; there is something very mystical about your persona. Besides, when one has to take important decisions like this, one goes for substance. You are more like what my mother was and what I would want my daughter to be like.'

Parvathi felt overwhelmed by this last bit that Anil said. By now, she was well and truly in love.

'I can't possibly say no. Yes I'll marry you.'

Anil rose from his seat, went around, took her hand and kissed her on the cheek. Parvathi blushed and felt embarrassed as other guests in the restaurant looked towards them.

Anil confessed that he had taken a fancy for her the very first time he saw her. Her eyes exuded a rare sincerity, something he had not seen in the other girls. On knowing her, he was glad that the eyes reflected the person she was.

Anil told her about his parent's search for a bride for him.

'My parents are concerned about my marriage. Though they haven't told me, I know they are looking for a suitable girl.' Anil said. 'But I don't think they would be successful.'

'Why?' asked Parvathi.

'Because I can't marry someone I don't know. I always liked to marry someone like you.'

'Anil, my parents have put an ad somewhere on internet and they keep looking for a boy. They are finicky about Kerala boy. I can't marry someone I am not sure about,' Parvathi answered.

They both looked at each other and smiled thinking they have already made their choice now.

Anil dropped her at South Extension where her car was parked in the parking lot. They kissed again and went home talking on their mobiles with speakers on. They had decided not to spring a surprise on their parents and wait for the right moment to disclose their preference in this matter.

'I would suggest we let them exhaust their options searching for a suitable partner for us,' Anil said. 'If I disclose my choice now, there is going to be enormous opposition to the very idea of marrying a south Indian girl.'

'I feel the same. It's better if they keep trying for someone from Kerala. Considering my qualifications, background and nature, I know it's not that easy to find one. Even if they find one, I'll simply not agree with their choice,' Parvathi agreed. 'I really don't understand my parent's preference for a south Indian boy.'

****

Anil being a Punjabi and Parvathi a Keralite, their opposite streaks of nature fuelled the mutual attraction between them. Anil liked her quite nature as much as she loved his assertiveness and talkative nature. She liked his flamboyance as he adored her simplicity.

The hurry to leave office in the evening was no more evident. On way back home, they stopped to have coffee either in Radisson Noida or Hyatt in Delhi. On Sundays, Parvathi and Anil managed to watch movies until their families started missing their absence and could not figure out the suddenness of change in their set schedule. It was only when Ritu was casually informed by one of her club members that Anil was seeing a girl on a regular basis that she felt deeply concerned and thought of sharing this information with her husband.

'Do you know Anil is going around with a girl?' Ritu said as Chawla Bhai came back after his regular spell of drinks in the club.

'*Punjabi puttar hai*. If not a girl, who would he go around with, a boy?' Chawla muttered.

'You don't understand. These girls are after my son. He is so naïve. I am not going to accept any *aisee waisee* girl in my family,' Ritu retorted.

By this time four large 'Patiala' pegs of whiskey had done its job.

Chawla Bhai, barely conscious, stammered, 'What's wrong with that? Didn't I accept you?'

It marked the beginning of a noisy scene.

Ritu fumed and pacing up and down said, 'I was such a big fool to have married you.'

'But I was in love so I didn't mind it.' Chawla Bhai muttered as he spread himself on the bed.

There was the familiar noise of glass breaking on the marble floor but Chawla Bhai was blissfully snoring.

The mornings in Chawla household never showed any traces of past evenings or early nights. No one ever talked about the drunken squabble of previous night. It was one of those mornings when Ritu convinced her husband about looking for a suitable match for Anil and giving an ad in the *Sunday Hindustan Times*.

****

Lathika lying in bed told Nair that it is time they should look for a suitable match for Parvathi. She shared her concerns about their daughter and mentioned that Delhi was different from California. She expressed her worry as Parvathi had started to come late from office and on Sundays she started going out with friends. Motherly instincts were emitting strong warning signals.

'Let's find a boy who is from our own land. I do not trust the north Indians,' Lathika said.

'What's wrong with them? We have lived here for almost thirty years now,' Nair enquired irritably.

'They are not straight like our boys and girls in Kerala. They usually pose different from what they are. I don't think I would like a north Indian son-in-law.' Lathika sounded resolute and convinced.

'I don't agree with your argument,' Nair thoughtfully said. 'Though I'll also prefer a boy from Kerala as our customs and habits are different from north Indians.'

Lathika felt relieved that her husband had agreed to look for a Kerala boy. She was not much bothered about his different reasons for doing so.

Being convinced about its urgency, Nair agreed to put an ad in the Keralamatrimony.com.

***

FOUR

'In love and on the battlefield timing your moves is as important as luck.' Her sister told her when Sheila Arora lost her boyfriend to her best friend in college. But her soaring ambitions and greed never allowed her to time her moves properly.

Shiela knew she was the hottest girl in the Company and men ogled at her and sought her company. She enjoyed expressing love openly in public places. But she was choosy and had an eye of an eagle for rich, successful and vulnerable men. Her growing interest for an unguarded Anil shifted the moment she spotted her next prey Rakesh Sharma park his father's Bentley and join Global Logix. One week later, she was sitting in her strap-less blouse in his Bentley while he explored her contours. 'Chasing a young, immature Anil occupying the lower rung of the Company ladder would be a waste of time,' Sheila thought. In contrast, Rakesh a married man loaded with money and with ten years of service in the Company's San Francisco branch behind him, looked highly attractive. Everyone knew Rakesh's marriage was on the rocks and he was available.

When Anil, Rakesh, other colleagues including Sheila went for a week-end conference in Goa, it was the tail-end of monsoon. The sky looked smoke grey and it was drizzling lightly as Rakesh and Sheila walked hand in hand along the parapet of the Taj Village.

'You are the first woman I've met who has balls, balls of steel. Maybe that's what keeps me interested in you,' said Rakesh.

'Shut up. I am your colleague and a friend. Don't over price yourself,' Sheila said, pinching his arm.

As they waded into the churning waters, a gigantic wave crashed against them. At this time of the year even local fishermen stayed on shore and mended their nets quietly. Sheila was amazed at herself. What was she doing with the unpredictable Rakesh- a brilliant software professional who has been consistently avoiding her request for divorcing his estranged wife living in US?

Sheila had grown fond of him and needed him both at work and play. They were waist deep in violently swirling water by now. Rakesh had a manic gleam in his eyes as he held on to her hand and pulled her deeper. Sheila's feet were sinking deeper into the rapidly moving sand. The rain had stopped. There was an eerie yellow glow in the overcast sky.

Rakesh pulled at her bikini clasp playfully. Sheila laughed in sheer fright. They could hear shrieks of laughter as a group of teenagers frolicked in the shadows.

'No one is looking. I swear.'

'No way, I can see our colleagues sitting on the wall looking at us. Anil and Rajesh are looking this way.'

She loved tantalizing Rakesh. It had started on the carpeted office floor when Rakesh and she tore off each other's clothes greedily to the sounds of nails being hammered in the adjoining room only few feet away. That was the first time. Since then it had become a pattern. She wondered how abandoned she could be and how uninhibited.

Sheila had found herself responding and craving for the chemistry created when they were together. She had stopped trying to analyze her out of character conduct with Rakesh.

Sheila and Rakesh discovered their hunger increase every day and thoughts about marriage and living together tormented them.

'I can't live without you Rakesh', Sheila said after every fiery encounter in their cottage in Goa. 'It's a heavenly feeling with you. Let's get married.'

'It's really an incredible sensation being with you. I can't think of a life without you any more,' Rakesh repeated as he took her in his arms again.

As they finished making love, Sheila allowed her mind to float. She blanked everything out- her work, her modest upbringing, her troubled past, but not her uncertain future. She realized the moment was here and now. She craved to be seen as the wife of a rich, successful and handsome hunk with the ferocious urgency she'd never experienced.

'Let's get married here in Goa.'

'I swear. I want you every day of my life,' Rakesh responded feeling her all over.

'I can't wait Rakesh. Let's marry here in some temple.'

'Let the marriage be in the usual style. Give me sometime, and we will be husband and wife honey. Meanwhile I have to sort out few complications.'

Sheila kissed him again, rested her head on his chest, imagined driving a Bentley from San Francisco to LA with Rakesh by his side playfully nibbling at her ear and fell asleep.

Their clandestine meetings continued in the Company office till Sheila sensed Rakesh's gradual loss of interest in her. The craving for the chemistry wasn't there any long.

Her attempts to attract his attention yielded no expected results. Her spaghetti straps, low cut front and exposed back failed to elicit the same sensual response from Rakesh. She failed in her analysis of Rakesh's changed behavior till she heard the office talk about his visiting American girl friend and his leaving for the San Francisco branch on transfer. But she didn't feel terribly disappointed as it wasn't the first time she experienced a failure in her attempts.

Being an ambitious woman in hurry, she had wrongly timed her earlier withdrawal from Anil. Now she realized her mistake of having spilt the milk when it could have been hers to drink and enjoy. The luring rich meadows of Rakesh also tricked her. Instead of crying over it, she started her overtures with Anil afresh.

Overcome by ambition and greed, had she not gravitated towards Rakesh at the last moment, she would have been able to entice Anil soon. She had earlier succeeded in gradually removing his wrappings one by one, exposing him to her predatory clutches. From coffee to lunches and dinner, movies to pecking and caressing in secluded corners, the progress had been painfully slow but steady. She was impressed by his height, muscular frame, his US background and his Mercedes. But Anil was painfully slow in responding to her demands on his time and had not shown his inclination to get into any kind of serious relationship and marry anyone in the near future. Had Sheila continued with her effort a bit more, who knows Anil might have succumbed to her charms? But she had different designs and went after Rakesh.

Her interest centered on Anil once more. It took few lunches, dinners and movies before she thought she could influence Anil about her unwavering friendship and loyalty towards him. But Anil, an expert in womanly manoeuvres, was determined to sail along playfully and make hay as long as the sun would shine. His stay in US had fortified him against the predatory tactics of females in the University. Anil played Sheila's own game skillfully and made her body, mind and soul writhe for him. He had seen her 'water games' with Rakesh on the beaches of Goa and had no feelings of attachment for Sheila left in him.

Timing her moves proved to be Sheila's biggest disadvantage again. She lost Rakesh as he went back to US and now Anil knew her game plan well. The moment he saw and befriended Parvathi he withdrew from Sheila though not as abruptly as she had dumped him for Rakesh before.

Parvathi, covered from neck to toe in her blouse and sari, quiet and shy, grabbed Anil's full attention who had no time for Sheila now. Parvathi's 'touch me not' approach lighting the fire in Anil made Sheila experience shame- shame about her body, her looks, her dress and practically every aspect of her life.

'A sex bomb's appeal lies in keeping the sex hidden. As a woman in a lingerie is considered desirable than a nude, when titillation descends into porn the mystique ends. Clever women rely on chaste titillation. That's what this south Indian bimbo is doing,' thought Sheila.

'You seem to have lost interest in me. Do you still feel something for me?' Sheila, unsure and concerned, asked Anil.

'Of course, I am your friend and shall always be,' Anil said avoiding her eyes.

'I don't think so. I know about your interest in that south Indian bimbo. Since you have had enough of me, it's time I would be thrown away like a waste paper.' Sheila flared.

'What rubbish. Isn't it like kettle calling the pot black? Who gives you all these insane ideas?'

'Insane? Have you talked to me once in last five days, leave aside touching me like before?'

'You know honey I have been busy.....'

'No you're not. Men like you classify women into two categories-available and unavailable. A girl wearing figure hugging costumes is considered loose and a girl who wears a sari appears unattainable and desirable. You found me represent natural beauty and bounty and my appeal transcend my statistics which aroused and inflamed you earlier. And now this saree clad plain and quite woman with a flower in her hair attracts you.'

'I think you are jealous of her,' Anil said.

'Yes I have to be. You no longer enjoy my company and I think we are drifting apart. Let me assure you of one thing honey. You are going to come back to my arms soon with your heart broken and your mind unsettled. I'll wait till this south Indian bombshell breaks your heart.'

'I think you need rest Sheila. You are talking nonsense.'

'Yes I need rest from you. You'll find me waiting for you round the corner whenever you are ready. You won't be able to find happiness with her. I'll haunt your mind and soul.'

Shiela walked out of Anil's office sobbing.

Sheila decided that she would not allow Anil, her last mascot to be snatched away from her. Anil made no effort to stop her, looked at her swaying back and wondered why she didn't excite him.

***

FIVE

It did not take long for Parvathi to sense her mother's inclination to arrange her early marriage.

She told Anil, 'you know, my parents were desperately looking for a suitable groom on internet. They want to fix up my marriage as soon as possible as my mother suspects I am dating someone.'

'Did she say anything?' Anil was alarmed.

'Not directly to me but I overheard her showing concerns to father about my coming late from office and going out on weekends.'

Anil had realized that they must have strong reasons to convince parents about their returning late every evening. For weekends, helping telephone calls from friends were required to go out and it meant sharing their secret with them. Rajesh and his wife were the best bet. Rajesh would call Anil's house in his absence and leave a message for joining him for lunch or a movie and his wife Radhika posing as Parvathi's friend would likewise take care of Parvathi's mother. The arrangement worked fine for few weeks, but the danger always seemed to be round the corner.

'Can't you tell them to wait for a year or so? I have to talk to my parents,' said Anil.

'Of course I will. But suppose they insist?'

'We will decide then.' Anil had no solution at hand.

****

Ritu unable to control her curiosity had asked Lovely to enquire from Anil about his marriage preferences, expecting if he had someone in mind, he would confide in his sister-in-law. When Lovely asked Anil, he assured her that he would like to wait for a year and marry someone chosen by the family.

Lovely had no reasons to believe him and asked, 'Who is the girl giving you regular company these days? Both of you have been seen together quite a few times. Can I also meet her?'

Anil was speechless for a moment as he had not anticipated such a question. He looked above as if in deep thought and making an effort to recollect the name of the girl.

'Oh, she is from the office and we are working together on a project. She is from Kerala. As she was in America for past few years and has just come back, I try to make her feel comfortable,' Anil lied, looking sideways.

'Mom feels something is brewing between the two of you. She is upset,' Lovely said, 'Do you really have to make her that comfortable?'

'I think Mom is imagining things,' Anil answered with a dismissive air.

'Let me tell you, Papa had placed an ad in the newspaper. Quite a few responses have come and they are being short-listed. Few phone calls have also have been received. It's not long before they finalize your alliance with someone,' Lovely confided.

Anil was totally in dark about this. He contemplated talking to his father, but after giving the idea a second thought, he decided against it.

He chose to discuss his problem with Rajesh Talwar, his friend in the office. Rajesh recently married the girl he loved. But by his words and actions no one presumed him to be so because of his tall, athletic physique, infectious, charming smile and ever ready flirtatious comments. The sight of a curvaceous female would evoke a strange, mischievous spark in Rajesh's behavior, typical of a college Romeo. Though he married his girlfriend yet he seemed bored with his marriage. His confidence level always soared high when he took alcohol. A highly self opinioned man, he had clarity of mind and never minced words.

Anil thought his friend could provide an objective and easy solution as he may have faced similar problems in his life earlier. For many weeks now, Rajesh and his wife had been bailing them out every weekend by calling their home and leaving messages for lunches, dinners or movies. Anil invited Rajesh for an evening out at Olive Bar in South Delhi.

Rajesh listened to Anil's predicament in complete silence as he downed pegs of whiskey and soda. After he got into his usual relaxed frame of mind, he blurted out.

'If you don't feel like marrying, why are you doing it? Let things remain as they are. Tell your parents you can't marry for another few years. There will be no fun after marriage.'

Anil was shocked by these words, especially coming from a newly married man.

Rajesh continued, 'Boss, last year my friend upgraded from Girlfriend 4.0 to Wife 1.0 and found that her memory hog left very little space and resources for other applications. Wife 1.0 installed itself in such a way that it monitors all system activity. Wife 1.0 leaves no scope for further installations. I should have gone for Wife 1.0 only after ensuring that she had an option to uninstall at anytime without loss of cache and other system resources. Another friend of mine decided to avoid the headaches associated with Wife 1.0 and stuck to Girlfriend 5.0. He also has problems. He discovered he could not install Girlfriend 6.0 over Girlfriend 5.0 as the uninstall option of Girlfriend 5.0 doesn't work well. It leaves traces of the application in the system. But worst of all, different versions of Girlfriends continuously send pop-up messages about the advantages of Wife 1.0. So, my dear Anil, marriage and girlfriends both have their advantages and disadvantages. Don't think too much about it,' Rajesh explained, drunkenly slurring his words.

Anil smiled at Rajesh's choice of computer jargon.

'But it's neither here nor there. What should I do?' Anil asked.

'Look mate; if you really love Parvathi then marry her. Don't wait for anything. Tell your folks. If you don't want to marry her and just want to have a good time with her before marriage then of course buy time.' Rajesh as usual, was clear in his thinking.

'*Tussi great ho*,' was all Anil could say to Rajesh.

By now Anil had made up his mind. He decided that there was no point waiting for a year or two. If he liked Parvathi he should marry her soon. One or two more years of bachelorhood didn't seem of any importance.

Anil called Parvathi and explained all options. She agreed with him that there is no point waiting and deceiving parents while they keep searching for prospective match in newspapers and on the internet. They decided to meet and discuss as soon as possible.

***

'I am thinking that we should get married. There is no point waiting for a year more. What do you suggest?' Anil asked Parvathi over dinner at Taj Palace.

'Last time you had mentioned about delaying it for a year so that you may talk to you parents. Why is this sudden change? Did you talk to anyone in your family?' Parvathi enquired.

'Not yet. There is no point waiting for more time as it's not going to change things.'

'So, what do you suggest?' Parvathi asked.

As the reality dawned on Anil and Parvathi about the complications involved in a north Indian- south Indian family wedding, Anil found himself as clueless as Parvathi. The sense of complacency gave way to a search for ways to address the issue of mutual acceptability of the two families.

'How should we go about it? My family is very much opposed to my marrying outside our community. What about yours?' Anil asked Parvathi.

'I suspect my mother is rigid about my marriage with a Keralite but Papa may not have a closed mind. I have never talked with either of them on this issue. But considering their nature I guess there would be hurdles which we have to cross jointly'. Parvathi thoughtfully explained as Anil watched the worried look on her face. They both remained silent for few minutes.

'How can I impress your parents, especially your mother? Is there a way you can suggest?' Anil asked. 'If I could satisfy their concerns about me, at least half of the battle would be won. With your assistance I shall try to take care of my parents.'

'I don't know how you can bridge the cultural differences. My mother hasn't changed despite twenty-five years of stay in Delhi. She doesn't like North Indian food, dresses like she used to earlier, thinks in Malayalam and then translates it into Hindi or English as the occasion demands, likes her own cuisine and is very orthodox in religious matters.'

'What else?' Anil asked.

'She has lived a simple life. She doesn't like to show off. She, in fact, hates those women who are talkative, social climbers, party types and hollow from inside.' Parvathi explained as Anil squirmed, thinking about his mother Ritu who had some of those traits which Lathika disliked.

'I'll try to address her concerns.' Anil said and his mind had already generated a plan.

On way home, Anil stopped at a book stall and bought books on Kerala cuisine, culture, society and tourism. He planned to go through all of them in a week and discuss the subtle nuances with Parvathi. Once armed with this ammunition in his arsenal he would invite her parents to dinner, finding a celebratory occasion where they would not hesitate to join.

After ten days of laborious reading, Anil managed to remember few facts about Kerala. He and Parvathi went to few restaurants serving Kerala cuisine and ordered only those dishes relished by her parents. Parvathi smiled, observing changes reflected in his facial features every time Anil helped himself with a portion of the dishes ordered. He ate *appam*, the soft rice flour pancake,*Aviyal*-a mixed vegetable gravy, *sambhar* and *rasam* to the delight of Parvathi who smiled all the time at his experiments. He tasted fish curry and found it tolerable. In all restaurants he had payasam, a dessert having milk, coconuts and cashew-nuts, at the end. He liked the dessert.

'How can you guys eat this? It's so weird?' Anil asked in the beginning.

'It's not weird. It's better than butter-chicken, '*makke di roti*' and '*sarson da saag*' or *Parathas* and *lassi* all the time.' Parvathi laughed loudly and teased Anil.

'I hope you won't force me to eat all this food?'

'No. I like both, north Indian food as well as Kerala food.' Parvathi tried to remove his concerns.

Next stop on Anil's journey towards learning about Kerala was its culture and dress. Parvathi told him about the dress common men wore in Kerala.

'Its *mundu* they wear with a shirt. It's something like a dhoti one wears in UP and Bihar but different.'

'Which is the famous dance form?'

'*Kathakali* is the dance where *katha* means the story and *kali* is the performance.'

Felling a bit frustrated about his progress of learning so far, Anil asked, '*Are yaar*, and is there anything significant about Kerala which I can remember easily?'

'Elephants are an integral part of Kerala life and perhaps a state symbol. *Kalaripayattu* is a kind of martial art in Kerala. Its literature is very old. Onam is the biggest festival.' Parvathi replied tersely, hoping Anil would at least remember few terms and their significance in Malayali life.

'Onam, I know. I know about the boat races as I have seen them on TV.' Anil mumbled and asked, 'Who are the modern writers in Kerala literature?'

'OV Vijayan, Sethu and our own Arundhati Roy *yaar*, one who wrote *The God of Small Things*. This novel was set in Kottayam town of Kerala and got the Booker prize.' Parvathi was suddenly excited remembering the Booker prize novelist.

Anil thought this knowledge must be good for a start though he wasn't sure about his ability to remember everything.

'When is Onam?' Anil asked.

'I believe it's on 12th September. Why?' Parvathi asked, suspecting Anil had something planned in his mind.

'Let's celebrate Onam in style. All Mallus in our company will be invited. I'll host a dinner party where parents will also be invited. But first let me find a place to host this party,' Anil said.

'Not a bad idea Anil. This way I can meet your parents also.'

'Yes,' Anil said, though he knew his parents wouldn't be there as he did not intend to invite them. He believed in one thing at a time. First he must make inroads into Nair's territory and make himself acceptable. Parvathi can meet them later.

Anil called Rajesh and coaxed and cajoled him to organize a party on Onam.

***

SIX

'*Bhayya*, you haven't told us anything about your girl-friend. You know, Mom and Papa have prepared a list of thirty girls. I have seen few photographs as well. They all looked so pretty.' Lovely told him one day, puzzled, not having heard anything further from Mom about Anil.

'What girl friend? I told you earlier I am not dating any one.' Anil replied, eying his sister-in-law suspiciously.

'Still, we all want to see you married soon. It really doesn't matter to me whether it's a love marriage or an arranged one.'

'It doesn't matter to me either. One is suicide, whereas other is arranged murder. Whether you fall in the well yourself or ten men arrange to push you in the well, it's one and same for me.' Anil tried to put her suspicions, if any, to rest.

'You mean to say you won't marry at all?' asked Lovely, a bit alarmed.

'When did I say that? When Mom, Papa and you guys find someone, inform me, I will marry that girl.'

Anil knew his mother won't find a girl so easily. She will always be on the lookout for still better and better. He needed few months of peace now, till he could dig a tunnel and enter the fortress of Adinath Ramchandran and Lathika Nair.

****

Rajesh arranged the Onam dinner party at Essex-Farm in Hauz Khas where twenty friends, colleagues and their parents were to assemble at 7 pm on 12th Sept. Parvathi along with Anil had visited the venue during the day and provided the finishing touches to the menu.

Nair, Lathika and Parvathi stepped out of their house to be greeted by Mrs. Bhasin's dog that sniffed at all three but fancied Nair most. Nair in anger kicked the dog as it tried to pull his 'mundu' but the dog caught the cloth in his mouth and pulled it so hard it gave way, torn at few places and exposing his unshapely legs. Cursing his neighbor, Nair refused to attend the Onam party but timely action from Lathika saved the evening for Anil and Parvathi. Lathika requested him to change into a fresh 'mundu', reminding him that the party was organized for Malayalis and the hosts would be disappointed if they didn't turn up. Nair unwillingly agreed, and as they came out the dog was still out in the open waiting for him with a piece of cloth hanging from its mouth. Nair was sure about it being a piece of his 'mundu'. He used his wife and daughter as his shield as Lathika *shooed* the dog away with a wave of her hand but it followed them right up to their car, his tail wagging. By then Nair had decided to mow down Mrs. Bhasin's dog under his car one day.

Anil was concerned as Parvathi had informed him about the mishap at home. He personally received the guests at the door. Nair apologized for the delay, explaining how his Punjabi neighbor had made his life difficult, while Anil flinched.

Parvathi came dressed in a traditional saree. Nair came wearing a *mundu* with a shirt. Anil thought it looked like a *lungi* which *Tamils* wear. But it was different and he could not make out the difference. Lathika was wearing a cotton saree with a big *tika* on her forehead and gold ornaments around her neck.

Anil accompanied them to the seating hall instructing Rajesh to welcome other guests.

Parvathi had arranged to get a flower mat made in the front. The Nairs liked the decoration and started mingling with other guests. Anil kept a safe distance from Parvathi as Lathika's eyes were not leaving her daughter for a minute. When all the guests had arrived, Anil was formally introduced to Nair and Lathika by Rajesh.

Nair said, 'It's so nice of all of you to celebrate this festival today. I thought young people have forgotten their roots and culture. It's a really a commendable effort Mr. Anil.'

'Thank you Sir, actually I like Kerala, the Land of the Gods, and its people.'

'Have you been there?'

'Yes Sir, few times. I had picked up a bit of *Kalaripayattu* also. Don't remember much now,' Anil said, as Parvathi who was listening to the conversation could not control her laughter and stepped back to hide her face.

It was Lathika's turn to be surprised now. She asked Anil, 'Are you from Delhi? You seem to be a Punjabi.'

'Yes I belong to Delhi, studied in US and always dreamt of working in Kerala. My closest friend in US was from Kerala. I still lick my fingers remembering Kerala dishes he used to prepare himself for all of us.'

'That's great. If you like Kerala cuisine that much, come over to our place, Lathika shall prepare it for you.' Nair looked at his wife proudly.

Before Anil could react, Lathika said, 'Yes why not? Who likes Kerala dishes here in Delhi? Nair hardly eats. And Parvathi, she eats sandwiches for lunch and fruits and yoghurt for dinner. This generation is so much weight conscious,'

'But I am not. I go to Lodi gardens for walk regularly. I do my exercises. I can eat whatever I like,' Anil replied.

'That's very good. I also go there every morning except on Saturdays and Sundays. Didn't see you, or maybe my memory is poor I say,' Nair remarked.

'I go there only on Saturdays and Sundays. During week days I have to leave for Noida very early.' Anil felt relieved at the opening provided by fate.

Anil thought it's time to move away for a while otherwise he would be caught on the wrong foot. Fate couldn't be kind all the time. He looked out for Rajesh who, hiding from others, had already downed a couple of pegs of whiskey. Anil snatched a peg from him and gulped it down to sooth his nerves. Parvathi's eyes followed him from a distance and she smiled.

Parvathi had arranged for the right choice of menu. *Thoran*, *avial*, banana, *sambhar*, *pachadi*, *fluffy idlis* and *appams* were there on the tables. Nair and Lathika savored the food and Anil and Parvathi could hear them appreciate the arrangements and the choice of menu.

'This boy is good and must be coming from a good family. Why aren't all Delhi boys like him? I want a Kerala boy for Parvathi with the same qualities.' Parvathi whispered to her husband.

Anil overheard her, smiled and thought, 'just wait Ma'am, till I come home for dinner. You won't even think about looking at others.'

As Nair, Lathika and Parvathi were leaving Anil led them to the gate, asked for the keys of the car and brought it from the parking lot. Nair shook his hands and profusely thanked him for the evening.

Anil folded his hands and said namastey to Parvathi who smiled and reciprocated in the same manner.

***

SEVEN

There were social occasions in Nair's home as his career required quite a few of them- and some were witnessed by Parvathi also. At them, Nair was pleased to indulge himself in a little whiskey and water. When he had done so, he began to make what his wife and daughter considered rather frightening attempts at jocularity. His jokes were mostly directed against others, and ferocious, under cover of geniality that seemed appropriate to the ambience of a dinner party or a club reception. Having made his guest squirm uncomfortably, he would laugh heartily. He measured the success of his jokes according to the amount of discomfort it caused others. One could be fooled into thinking that Nair was in good spirits. But his daughter was not fooled: she knew her father was rattled, shaken by what he saw as an obstacle to his rise in his profession. Parvathi was relieved when her father returned to taciturnity which was normal for him.

If one ever had occasion to go to Nair's office, he would be found sitting at an immense desk like the leader of some small provinciality, mopping his neck with a large handkerchief, giving curt orders to his secretary, his typist and his clients, every gesture and grimace adding to the carapace of his authority.

He had very few complaints in life; the top of the list was one against his Indian Administrative Service bosses whom he had served diligently all these thirty years. He attributed his stagnation in career to the sinister designs of his bosses. His second grouse was against his neighbor Mrs. Bhasin and her dog. He wished to see the dog dead and was sure he'd kill the dog soon.

In all these years he had come across only two bosses who empathized or commiserated with him. When one of them sent his son's proposal for his daughter, Nair was caught in a fix.

'Gupta Sahib has asked for his son Parvathi's hand in marriage. You know, his son has just graduated from Indian Institute of Management, Ahmedabad.' Nair told Lathika.

'What's his son doing now?'

'He works for Standard Chartered Bank in Mumbai,' Nair replied.

'Good. But, is he the one who was quite plump and balding four years back when we met him?' Lathika enquired.

'Yes. Gupta has only one child.'

'I don't think Parvathi would like that boy. Last four years must have further reduced his crop of hair,' Lathika smiled and said.

'How does it matter? The boy is working for a good international bank. He is the only child of his parents and they are known to us,' Nair said. 'There is no demand for dowry or anything. The proposal came from Mr. Gupta who is a gentleman, I say.'

'But, what about finding a Malayali boy?' Lathika asked. 'Are you happy with a north Indian UP type family of Mr Gupta?'

'What's wrong with a UP family if the boy and his parents are nice people and they suit us?' Nair asked. 'Let's ask Parvathi before we make up our mind.'

Nair and Lathika told Parvathi who refused to entertain any thought of marrying the Gupta boy. She remembered this young man vividly and shuddered at the mere thought of spending her life with him.

'Mom, he might have graduated from IIM or Timbuctoo but I know him since long. Earlier he was in Delhi and we met in parties. He seemed quite unlike me in thinking, taste and outlook,' Parvathi said. 'I am not marrying his family. My primary concern is the man with whom I have to spend my life.'

'But.......'

'I am sorry Papa. I can't marry someone I don't know at all. In this case, I know this gentleman and I don't like him a bit.'

Nair realized that his kingdom does not extend beyond the frontiers of his office room. Lathika was not with him in this matter. Parvathi had also decided that she can not be smothered by the wishes of her parents and their liking.

****

'Hi, Rekha, long time no see. What's up? You seem to have forgotten your old friend.' Parvathi called her after a gap of two months.

'You have become too big after coming back from America. I am the same, running a small institute and earning my bread and butter,' Rekha said. She asked sarcastically, 'what good have I done to deserve a call from Parvathi Madam today?'

'*Are yaar,* I apologize for not calling you earlier. Actually my job is such. I leave early for Noida and by the time I come back I am too tired for anything. You don't know, every Sunday I had been planning to visit you but something or the other cropped up. I want to come over in case you are free,' Parvathi said.

In thirty minutes Parvathi was sitting in the small but elegantly furnished office of Rekha Arora, Director of School of Fashion Designing, Vasant Vihar, New Delhi.

'So, how is life treating you? *Chal Bataa* what's new in your life?' Rekha asked.

'Rekha darling, I am in love with a Punjabi *munda*, your community baby. I want to marry him.'

'*Great yaar*, when did this happen? You kept me in dark. Now I understand why you didn't get time?'

'It's not that. We work in the same company in Noida. Like me, he was in US earlier though we never met each other there. I came, I saw and I conquered him. We liked each other and fell in love. Now we want to get married.'

'*Chat mangni pat byah*, so fast? Show me his photo. When do I meet him?' Rekha asked impatiently.

Parvathi told Rekha about Anil, his parents and their preference for a girl from their community. Though Rekha knew about Parvathi's parents and their fondness for everything belonging to Kerala which included a son-in-law, Parvathi told her about the chance meeting of Anil with her parents at Essex Farms during Onam. She explained how Anil could manage to impress her parents and earned an invitation to dine at their home.

'I also need such a break *yaar*. I want to meet Anil's parents and make an impression on them before they find out more about me.' Parvathi implored.

'Sure you do. But I don't know how you would manage that.'

'I know that. You can arrange it if you want.'

'I'll cross Himalaya for you baby. Tell me what I have to do,' Rekha said.

Then Parvathi explained the entire plan. Rekha was supposed to organize an exhibition of modern fashion designs created by students in the Institute at a swanky venue. Rekha would then invite Anil's parents. Mrs. Ritu Chawla, Anil's mother would be the Chief Guest and her husband be the guest of honor. During the event Rekha would introduce Parvathi as the sole spirit behind the event.

'Why should Ritu Chawla agree to be the chief guest?' Rekha asked.

'Elementary Dr Rekha; because of the fact she is a social climber, she would pledge her soul to be the chief guest at such an event. You have to just handle her skillfully. Just a phone call would do. Try it now,' Parvathi eagerly explained and scribbled her phone number on a piece of paper and passed on.

'And where do we organize an event like this? Do you know it will take at least fifteen days to host an event like this?'

'I know. We'll book a hall in Habitat. We'll manage that. Fifteen days is ok,' Parvathi said.

'By the way, who are we?'

'Oh. It's me and Anil. He is with me in this.'

Rekha burst out laughing.

'Great. Let's call the social flier now and see what she says.' Rekha started dialing Ritu's number as Parvathi intently waited.

'Hello, May I speak to Mrs. Ritu Chawla?'

'Speaking.'

'Good heavens. I can't believe my luck that I am talking to the great and famous socialite of Delhi Mrs. Ritu Chawla herself. Actually I am Rekha, Director of Institute of Fashion Designing, calling to invite you Ma'am for our exhibition of designs and fashion designer clothes at Habitat next month.

Our students want you to be the chief guest on this occasion and bless them with your vision about future. I have heard and read so much about you that it would be a personal dream come true.' Rekha winked at Parvathi and waited for Ritu's response.

'It's so kind of you to invite me. I have plans to go to Paris next month for a fashion show. You must know Rita Beri. She wants me to be a guest at her fashion show there. But maybe I'll have to modify my schedule now. You know, I always believe in encouraging our local talent. Have you fixed a date or is it flexible?'

'Ma'am we take the convenience of the chief guest. You'll be the chief guest so you tell us which date shall suit you?' Rekha winked again at Parvathi.

'Any date during second week next month will be finc.' Ritu was free the whole month but she knew she must express her precise availability and unavailability.

'Is 11th October fine? It's Saturday. At five PM. I shall send the formal invitation.'

'Suits me fine.'

'Ma'am we would like to invite Mr. Chawla also as a guest of honor. The event will be followed by cocktails and dinner,' Rekha added.

'Yes. He will come. Good you have organized cocktails. By the way, may I also invite few of my friends from different clubs? Mr. Chawla can also invite few of his friends.' This was the opportunity Ritu had longed for all her life. Now her relatives, friends and neighbors would come to know about her talent and stop bitching.

'No issues Ma'am. It will give us pleasure. I'll send fifty blank invitation cards you can distribute amongst your friends,' Rekha agreed and hastily added, 'I can send more if you need.'

'Thanks fifty will do. Thank you Rekha, I have made a note of the date and time. We'll be there. Bye'

Parvathi and Rekha hugged and kissed each other. They were overjoyed.

'What a great actress you are Rekha? Never knew you can be so authentic while talking,' Parvathi exclaimed.

'Anything for you Ma'am but before next week, give me a cheque of Rs Twenty-five thousand and don't forget to book the hall for 11th October. Ask Anil to arrange bottles of beer and whiskey otherwise it will cost you more,' Rekha laughed and told Parvathi.

'Here is the cheque for twenty five thousand rupees.' Parvathi took out her cheque book and wrote a cheque and said, 'Don't forget to mention I am the woman behind the show, and yaar say a lot in my praise. You are a real darling Queen.'

The first call went to Anil. Parvathi told him everything. He was excited but sighed when told that he couldn't accompany his parents to the show as it wasn't for single males though he could sneak in on some other pretext.

He felt relieved as he already knew how he could be present there.

****

Ritu made more than fifty phone calls informing all her friends, relatives and in case they were unavailable, their spouses and children. Wanting to break the news personally, she waited for Chawla Bhai to return home.

'You know I have been invited to be the chief guest at a fashion show organized by The Institute of Fashion Designing on 11th October. You are also invited and I have promised them you are coming.' Ritu told him.

'That's a pleasant surprise. Why have they chosen you? Never heard about you being the chief guest at any fashion show before?' Chawla Bhai seemed genuinely surprised and added, 'The organizers must be having some hidden selfish motive.'

'You always underrated me and my standing in the eyes of the people. *Ghar di kudi* is never important. What hidden interests could they have? We are not from their line of business. You all seem unable to digest my success. You find it difficult to appreciate how your wife is known all over Delhi,' Ritu feeling hurt, retorted.

'I know *how* well known you are?' Chawla Bhai muttered pouring his whiskey in the glass, and to end the conversation said, 'Anyway, congratulations'.

'Thank you. It's followed by cocktails and dinner. I have got fifty blank invitation cards for my club friends. They would attend the show with husbands. It's a great honor to be the chief guest in the presence of friends and well-wishers. Promise me you would come.' Ritu came close and pleaded.

'Yes *my title* I will'. Chawla Bhai caressed her back.

****

Rekha and Parvathi planned a brief and rough outline of the event. Rekha would welcome the guests and introduce Parvathi to the audience which would be basically Ritu's friend circle as Rekha was organizing the show for Ritu. Only ten girls from the Institute would walk on the ramp. There would be a visual show of latest designs prepared by the Institute in the recent past.

'Are you sending invites to other designers and guests in your list you invite regularly?' Parvathi asked.

'No way, I don't want to be ridiculed by my own people. Who knows this Ritu Chawla *yaar*? I am just doing it for you honey. The audience would be Ritu's friend circle. She can have as many invitation cards as she wants,' Rekha said.

'But how are you going to introduce me?' Parvathi asked.

'Leave that to me. Let's keep it as a surprise. You concentrate on your presentation speech.' Rekha assured her.

***

EIGHT

Exactly at thirty minutes past five in the evening of 11th, October, Ritu and her husband Chawla Bhai stepped out of their Mercedes car. Chawla Bhai was in a grey suit and blue neck tie and Ritu was wearing a purple chiffon designer saree with a blouse that revealed more than it covered. Parvathi and Rekha did not take any moment to recognize them as Parvathi knew their car like the back of her palm. Quite often, Anil used this car to ride to office.

Rekha introduced herself and Parvathi; handed over the flower bouquets and led them to the main hall where the guests had already assembled.

After lighting the lamp and when everyone was seated, Rekha took the mike and said, 'It's our privilege to have Mrs. Ritu Chawla with us this evening. She is a connoisseur of changing fashion designs in the country, a widely traveled woman and a member of the elite clubs of Delhi. I really thank my friend Parvathi who suggested her name and coaxed me to request Ritu *ji* to be the chief guest. I am extremely thankful to Ritu *ji* for sparing her valuable time for us. I also welcome Mr. Chawla, her debonair husband who could find time for us from his hectic schedule.'

Chawla Bhai looked at the audience, waved his hand seeing familiar faces around and was enjoying moments of reflected glory.

Rekha explained briefly the theme of the event and the difference between fashion designing and costume designing, and changing ready-to-wear and mass market. She mentioned about the designing activities within their Institute and the theme of the show.

While introducing Parvathi to the audience, she said, 'I have with me, my friend Parvathi, who is not a designer by vocation but has a keen eye for fashion designing industry and who helped us in the application of Information Technology in fashion designing. She was in US and has now joined a multinational company in India. When we thought of organizing this event, Parvathi offered to guide us and told us about a specific lady she had in mind, though she had not met her personally. She had heard about Ritu Chawla *ji* and seen her beautiful photographs on page three of various newspapers. That's why we chose the theme of our autumn/winter *haute couture* designs keeping Ritu *ji* in our mind. The theme is 'Women's Evening Wear' for the glamorous, sophisticated and apt women like Ritu Chawla. After meeting Ritu, I can only thank Parvathi for such a correct and timely advice.'

Ritu looked at her husband conceitedly and then at the audience and smiled, enjoying her glorious moments.

The catwalk was about to begin when Ritu asked Parvathi sitting next to her, 'When did you come from America? It's a nice show you have organized. I am extremely thankful to you for keeping me in mind. Have we met before? Your face looks familiar.'

Parvathi lied that she met her once in Gymkhana club and remembered her elegant dress and beautiful face.

'I am surprised that you remembered me and invited me. I keep very busy and this time I had to refuse Rita Beri's offer to go to Paris and Milan. But I shall be a part of Lakme fashion week being organized from 20th Oct in Mumbai. We must meet later.'

'Yes Ma'am,' was all Parvathi could say, her thoughts being numb.

'Are you from Delhi?'

'No. I have lived here for last twenty five years. I am originally from Kerala,' Parvathi replied with hesitation and watched Ritu's expressions.

'But you are very pretty and don't look or speak like a Keralite. No one can guess you are not from Delhi.'

'It's because our family has stayed in Delhi for more than thirty years.' Parvathi looked into her eyes and replied.

'Thank you Parvathi. Here is my card, call me later. We must meet.' Ritu said.

Parvathi was satisfied with the progress so far and soon the music started and girls started coming one by one on the ramp.

The 'Generation Next' and 'Emerging Designer' category showed amazing collection of designs prepared by girls in the Institute. An evening *haute couture* collection, flavor of the *crème de la crème* and urban rich women like Ritu Chawla was influenced by both Indian traditional values and the new and fast paced modern life. It was followed by the ancient practice of *Shringar*, or the art of adornment.

The hall resounded with claps every now and then.

Chawla Bhai's eyes roamed around looking for the drinks stall which was being set up.

Ritu was transported to her dream world. She had been the star attraction of the event. She knew that she would have to come on stage to say something and thank the organizers therefore she had come prepared remembering the names of leading designers and few fashion design terms. Ritu believed in doing spade work.

Ritu thanked Rekha and the models who presented her collection. But she reserved her highest adulation for Parvathi.

'No words are sufficient to express my feelings for the young and wonderful lady Parvathi who is the soul of this evening. She is sophisticated, intelligent, immensely talented and very much a Delhite like all of us. After talking to her I feel that she is in the wrong line of work; she should be a designer herself rather than assisting Rekha *ji* in pattern making and styles through her IT skills. I feel she has the potential to become a leading branded designer herself like Calvin Klein, Ralph Lauren or Chanel. She is a keen observer of changing patterns in designs. I am pleasantly surprised that she remembered my dresses worn earlier. You all know I am fond of designer dresses to keep up with the changing times and try to express myself through styles and colors. Let me present a cheque of Rs One hundred thousand to Rekha *ji*, the Director of this Institute.' She said.

Chawla who was lost in thought, suddenly squirmed and shifted in his seat and before he could realize what had hit him he heard claps all around him. He sheepishly nodded in agreement.

Rekha and Parvathi had thought Ritu would be a brainless bimbo, a smug and self absorbed idiot loaded with money having no knowledge of fashion industry. But practice had made Ritu perfect and she couldn't have acted any better. Ritu smiled when she was required to smile, lighted the lamp with just the right touch of reverence, stood stock still for the photographs, didn't flinch from the flashbulbs popping in her face, shook hands with the demureness of a princess and handled the fashion designers around her with the sangfroid of a fellow celebrity.

****

Chawla felt cheated. He had known his wife's penchant for misplaced generosity borne out of self adulation. But since he was being congratulated by everyone he kept quiet. But after few drinks down his parched throat, he was his usual self.

Someone from his wife's social circle congratulated him and asked, 'Chawla Bhai what's bugging you? It's only one hundred thousand rupees she has donated to the Institute and being a millionaire it's nothing for you.'

Chawla said, 'I was a billionaire before I married her. At this rate I would not even continue to be a millionaire.'

His neighbor's wife also present in the hall congratulated him and said, '*Bhaisaheb*, Ritu spoke so well. She is a real angel.' Chawla could not hide his anguish and said 'But she is very much alive,' and grimly walked to refill his glass.

Anil his son, who had sneaked in when his mother was making her speech, tried to cheer him up. Anil sensing his foul mood told him that their photos would be splashed on page three in the newspapers and whole of Chandni Chowk would feel jealous of them. Chawla Bhai had some advice for him also, 'you know son; man is incomplete before he marries. After marriage he is finished.'

Whiskey and his son's presence soothed his nerves. Ritu joined her husband and introduced Rekha to him again. Chawla Bhai with a usual slur in his voice complimented her and her team for the splendid show. Ritu brought Parvathi with her and told her husband that she intended to work closely with her.

On seeing Anil in the hall, Ritu was pleasantly surprised and introduced him to Rekha and Parvathi. She told Anil how Parvathi had casually met her earlier and still remembered her and her dress. Rekha, Parvathi and Anil found it hard to stop smiling. Ritu kept Parvathi with her during dinner.

She asked her, 'Where do you work Parvathi?'

'I work for Global Logix in Noida,' Parvathi said, fearing that Ritu would certainly be surprised since her son also worked there.

'What a coincidence. Anil, my son also works there. You just met him. Haven't you two met before?' Ritu asked.

'I am afraid, no. I am not very old in the Company and there are so many people working there with different working hours.' Parvathi managed a reply.

Ritu waved to Anil to come closer. She asked Anil, 'You work in the same company as Parvathi. It's strange you don't know her?'

Anil an expert in ducking such questions said, 'we don't get time to mix with each other. I do feel now that I have seen her before. Hmmm.... What's your name? Yes, you said Parvathi.'

When Parvathi had left to join Rekha, Ritu scolded him for ignoring such a talented and elegant girl. 'These boys have no discerning ability these days and have no taste for good things' Ritu thought.

Ritu told Chawla Bhai who was listening silently to the conversation, 'see how Anil has changed after coming back from US. He can't differentiate between an elegant, sophisticated girl and an average girl. He has been seen going around with someone and doesn't know about girls like Parvathi working in the same building.'

Chawla Bhai, an old experienced Casanova himself and a man of great intuitive feelings smiled, as if he had suddenly discovered the principles of gravity before Newton did.

'*Puttar*, you can't fool your father. After all you are a son of a Punjabi, who can fool others. Parvathi must be *the* girl you are dating and your presence today explains it,' he mused.

But he chose not to share his intuition with his wife as he wasn't completely sure.

***

NINE

Anil and Parvathi decided to take lunch at La Piazza in Hyatt Hotel. It was time Anil must meet her parents, Parvathi thought.

Though her parents had asked Anil to come home, yet a formal invitation seemed necessary and had not gone so far. Parvathi had been busy with the preparations for the show at Habitat and didn't want Anil to be invited during that time. She had succeeded in making a mark on Anil's parents but now they needed to move further, she thought.

During a family dinner at home, she raised the subject of Onam celebrations at Essex farm on 12th Sept, hoping her parents would remember that they had earlier invited Anil to come over for a home cooked Kerala meal. But it evoked no response from either of her parents and it seemed as if they had completely forgotten about the entire event and extending an invitation to Anil.

In desperation she fired another salvo.

'You cook so well, Mom. Why don't we invite friends from my office for an authentic home made food? You should let your culinary skills be known to everyone.'

'No one likes Kerala cuisine here. I had invited so many of your father's colleagues earlier. They were polite on my face and appreciated our food but I knew they didn't relish it, except those, who were from Kerala and other southern States.' Lathika complained.

'I don't know about father's office colleagues, but my colleagues in the office do like Kerala food. I have seen so many of them visiting south Indian restaurants. Don't you remember how one of my colleagues appreciated the food which was served on 12th Sept? Believe me; the young generation of ours is very discerning in our food habits and we like to experiment with various types of cuisine unlike father's colleagues who might have fixed likes and dislikes about food.' Parvathi pressed further.

'Why don't you invite few friends on one of these holidays? Your papa would be home.' Lathika asked.

'Thanks Mom. I would only invite the ones you and Papa had invited yourself.' Parvathi reminded them at the right time.

'Yes, I completely forgot. What's his name? hmmmmm, don't remember now. He must be wondering what type of persons we are.'

'Anil.' Parvathi immediately provided the name.

Lathika looked at the calendar and fixed the date of the dinner. Parvathi decided that she would invite Anil alone. Other friends like Rajesh could wait for some other time.

Anil was not exactly overjoyed by the prospects of having lunch or dinner at Nair's house. Though he badly wanted to come close to them, yet the thought of a home cooked authentic Kerala meal didn't seem very exciting. He was more concerned about his encounter with Parvathi's parents. He reverted back to the books on Kerala, gathering dust on the table in his study. Frustrated with reading books, he thought of a better course of action.

Anil became convinced that he must visit Kerala to gain first hand knowledge and should not merely depend on knowledge gained through books and visits to restaurants. He decided that Parvathi must also be with him and he should try to see Kerala through her eyes. 'Heaven's would not fall if the dinner meeting with Parvathi's parents is postponed for a few more days,' he thought.

A job related tour was easily planned by both, independently. Except Anil and Parvathi, no one either in office or at home knew they were to travel together.

****

Chawla Bhai had been spending sleepless nights for last one week. He had not shared his problem with either Ritu or his eldest son Amit. His worries revolved around the matrimonial advertisement for Anil in *Hindustan Times*. He didn't seem to have any solution ready at hand.

Chawla Bhai had short listed seven matrimonial proposals for Anil. Only five out of the seventy proposals he received in response to the newspaper advertisement, did he find attractive and worth following up. The other two had come from known sources-one from his friend in Daryaganj and another from his daughter-in-law Lovely's family.

One proposal not in his list of probable candidates but cause of his sleepless nights had come from Patna. A gentleman named Angad Singh from Patna had sent the bio-data of his daughter studying in Jawaharlal Nehru University, Delhi. Angad Singh was a criminal turned known politician from the state of Bihar. Chitra was his only daughter with five brothers. Angad Singh had brazenly suggested a Rs Ten Crore pompous wedding in his initial proposal itself which also contained a veiled threat. It said that his daughter had liked the profile of Anil, his mother Ritu and the family background, and thought she would be happy to enter into a matrimonial alliance with Anil. Being his darling daughter, Angad Singh ji had never deprived her of anything. To keep her happy he might move mountain and earth.

Chawla Bhai thought he was caught between the devil and the deep sea. He couldn't consider a criminal's daughter as his daughter-in-law, even for a moment. Money alone couldn't attract him. But a refusal at this stage might invite some kind of retribution from the criminal turned politician.

Sitting in Delhi Gymkhana, Chawla Bhai shared his predicament with his friend Om *ji* Arora, another frequent visitor in the Gymkhana Club. Om *ji* had solutions to all kind of problems, even personal, when he consumed three pegs of his favorite Black-label whiskey. A pot bellied and balding merchant from Azad Market, with each gulp of alcohol Omji's brain cells became hyper-active and at times produced stunning solutions in a very desultory manner.

Delhi Gymkhana club spread over twenty seven acres of prime land in the heart of Lutyen's New Delhi and one of the oldest and elite clubs of Delhi had one regular visitor, Chawla Bhai. He liked its ambience, the Chinese restaurant 'Chopsticks' and the beautiful landscapes of the Woodland lawns. Fifteen days a month he dined at the club tasting variety of cuisines from Indian and Chinese to Hyderabadi, Thai and sea-food prepared by the professional chefs of the club. Chawla was an old member of the club. Though the club had premier sporting facilities, he was only interested in the bar and dining hall activities.

'What's the problem *yaar*?' Omji asked, making light of the entire issue bothering his friend.

'Haven't I told you what it is? I can't have a daughter-in-law from a criminal family even if they offer me one hundred crores or one hundred billion rupees for my son.' Chawla Bhai was visibly irritated. 'And refusal may also invite his wrath. He is a criminal turned politician,' he added.

'Why should you refuse?' Omji said, downing his fifth patiala peg of Black label.

'Are you out of your mind?' Chawla wanted to kill his friend sitting opposite him.

'Relax, I mean why you should refuse. Ask for the girl's horoscope. We would say it doesn't match.' Omji made an effort to calm him.

'I don't want to write to this Angad Singh or whatever.' Chawla moaned.

'Ok. Leave that to me. Just give me his address. I will correspond with him.' Om*ji* made an effort to rise from his chair but slumped back. He was carried to his chauffer driven Honda Accord, as always.

Omji's letter to Angad Singh ji asking for the horoscope of the girl in fact had the opposite effect and expedited the matter.

****

Four Tata Safari SUVs stopped at the front door of Chawla Bhai's show-room. A tall, square faced, muscular man with long moustache and dressed in white kurta-pyjama entered the shop followed by four gun wielding followers. Others stayed outside. The expectation of attending to a rich and important customer vanished in thin air the moment the entrant identified himself as the eldest son of Angad Singh of Patna. He asked for Chawla Bhai whose interest in the young man had turned into concern, touched his feet and handed over the horoscope of his sister.

Angad Singh's son with folded hands said, '*Tauji*, it's so nice you asked for my sister's horoscope. My sister is also non-manglic and our family astrologer has predicted a good match for her. Anil *ji's* horoscope is bound to match with hers. When can we all come over and discuss the matter further?'

Chawla Bhai had no answer. He wanted to pull out his hair in frustration. He cursed Omji with choicest abuses in his vocabulary.

'Beta, we shall let you know. Someone from our side will see your father soon.' Chawla, his senses numb, as if he had a seen a ghost right before his eyes, couldn't think of any other reply.

Attending to thc ring on his mobile, the unexpected visitor suddenly got up, touched Chawla Bhai's feet again, as he flinched, and said, 'Thank you Tau *ji*, I need to rush. I have to reach UP Bhawan on Sardar Patel road as someone is waiting for me. Sorry to be leaving so soon, *tauji*.'

'*Tauji* my foot,' Chawla muttered.

Chawla Bhai started dialing Om*ji*'s mobile. He wanted to abuse him with all the strength and intensity at his command, and for long.

'*Idiot*, what have you done? You are a first rate idiot. Now they have sent me her horoscope and they claim it will match my son's horoscope. What am I supposed to do now?'

'Chawla Bhai, what's the matter? Calm down. What have I done? What are you talking about?' Om*ji* Arora was really confused.

'You fool, I followed your advice and now I am in a soup.' Chawla stammered in anger.

'Bhai, how can you be in a soup? I know you must be joking. You enjoy your foam bath in the tub. I really don't understand what you mean by saying you are in a soup. Or is it soap you mean?' asked Om*ji*, still confused by the way Chawla was talking.

'You stupid, Angad Singh's son came with his musclemen. He gave me his sister's horoscope. He claims that it will match Anil's horoscope. It's you who suggested this step. Now they are expecting a response from our side. You have really created a big problem for me.' Chawla Bhai, a bit mellowed by now, explained.

'Not a big deal Chawla Bhai. Let's meet at Gymkhana in the evening. I will find a way out. Don't bother at all. Leave it to me.'

Om*ji*'s words always had a confident air about them and they soothed Chawla's nerves.

They met at Gymkhana at half past nine and in half an hour Om*ji* removed fears from Chawla Bhai's heart. During thirty minutes Om*ji* made three calls from his mobile. One call was made to Angad Singh.

He assured Chawla that next morning he will fly to Patna and settle the issue once and for all. Chawla felt relieved and had two more pegs as he knew Omji was such a smooth talker he could sell a drowning man a glass of water.

****

Om*ji* reached Patna by noon as his flight got delayed by an hour. He called Angad Singh's residence and was told to come home at four in the afternoon.

Om*ji* took bath and had lunch. He hired a taxi for Angad Singh's residence in Civil Lines. The drive took almost thirty minutes till the big name plate outside Angad Singh's gate was visible from quite a distance.

Om*ji*, undeterred by the presence of half a dozen gun trotting muscle-men outside, announced his arrival. He was immediately ushered in.

As he waited in the drawing-room for the mafia turned politician to arrive, he looked at family photographs on the wall. It didn't take him long to identify Angad Singh's daughter Chitra in the photo. She looked very much like her father minus his moustache. She seemed a well fed and pampered kid. Omji marveled at the costly wall hangings and chandeliers.

'*Pranam* Om*ji*. I hope your journey was comfortable,' Angad Singh said while entering the room.

Om*ji* was taken aback. He had not heard any footsteps and was in deep thoughts. He looked at Angad Singh's tall frame and long moustache and wondered how many persons he had possibly 'liquidated' so far.

'Namastey *ji*. I am sorry to have come at such a short notice. The matter is urgent.' Omji made his opening remarks.

'Please be seated. What can I do for you?' Angad Singh asked while indicating his men in his customary manner to bring tea.

'My son works for a Multi-national company in Gurgaon. He has seen your daughter in Jawaharlal Nehru University and has requested me to contact you in this reference. Initially I was a bit hesitant as someone informed me that you have already found a match for her. But upon further enquiry I found out that it's my neighbor's son Anil who is being considered for Chitra, your daughter.'

Om*ji* waited for some reaction from Angad Singh whose face showed no expression. The long moustache hid whatever little changes his facial muscles could produce.

Om*ji* continued. 'I thought why I should poke my nose in this matter. After all, my neighbor Chawla has been continuously trying hard to get his son married. He is willing to spend any amount to get a good daughter-in-law. Then I thought there is no harm in approaching you for my son. You know matrimonial alliances are made in heaven. We merely follow them here.'

Angad Singh who was listening attentively suddenly asked, 'Why Chawla ji should be worried about his son? He is well settled, smart and young. In Bihar it's the girl's father who spends money on his daughter not the father of a son.'

'Oh, you don't know? Chawla's son was in America. He met with an accident and damaged his spine. That's not a big issue. More serious is the fact that his injury has made him impotent. Very few persons know this. After all, how can Chawla proclaim it from roof top? That's why he is willing to spend any sum of money to see his son married. He has to keep his nose intact.'

Om*ji* had played his trump-card and looked at Angad Singh.

But this time he could clearly see lines of worry turning into frown and then anger on his face. The long moustache failed to hide the deepening furrows.

'How do you know this?' He asked Om*ji*.

Omji decided to be cautious now as he had made the desired impact. He should not sound very much definite and privy to this information.

'My information is based on hear-say, Angad Singh *ji*. Chawla's close friends know this. When his son met with an accident Chawla had to rush and on his return he confided to a few friends that though his son could survive, the serious spinal injury has made him impotent. I have no means to verify this. You can understand it Angad Bhai,' Om*ji* said.

'Quite right, how can anyone know for sure? But Chawla should not advertise in the newspapers so openly about his son. He has no right to deceive people. You *Dilli-Walaas* are like that. You have his telephone number?' Angad asked.

Omji had come prepared. He passed a slip of paper with Chawla's mobile number on it and waited for the inevitable.

'Chawla, you are a real cheat. I responded to your advertisement in the newspaper, my son met you and you didn't have the ethical sense to tell us about your son's handicap? Had it not been for your neighbor Om*ji*, I would have pushed my daughter in the well. You guys have no morality left in you. You don't think about spoiling a girl's future. Thank your stars that I came to know before hand, otherwise I would have butchered you and thrown your pieces in the forest…….. I'll get posters printed and news splashed on the walls of your son's office and in your entire Chandni Chowk.'

As Angad Singh was shouting on his mobile Om*ji* relished the home made pakoras and *masala*-tea and wondered how many pieces of Chawla would have been made by Angad and his men and how.

After Angad was finished with Chawla Bhai and exhausted, he turned to Om*ji*.

'Though I am thankful to you for sharing this information with me I can not think of marrying my dear daughter to any 'Delhi based crook'. I am happy with my people here and will look for a suitable match for her in the neighborhood or in my known circle of friends. I would never trust the newspaper advertisements.'

Om*ji* was relieved and felt that he should not give up easily as Angad may later try to check up his story.

'Angad Singh *ji*, everyone is not like Chawla. Moreover, who knows I may be wrong. I have only heard the facts from people. You may enquire from doctors in US in case you wish to.' Omji said only to remove any lurking suspicion Angad Singh might have on him. He knew that it is beyond the capability of Angad Singh to verify anything from doctors in America.

Om*ji* had succeeded in planting the seeds of doubt in Angad Singh's mind. The matrimonial alliance with Chawla became history now. Angad Singh had no interest left to prolong this conversation.

Angad Singh rose from his chair and said *namastey* and walked back into the adjoining room without even looking at Omji. Om*ji* hastily reciprocated and drove back in the taxi waiting outside to the airport for his flight to Delhi.

On the way he called Chawla from his mobile who received him at Delhi airport and in high spirits they both drove to Gymkhana for their quota of spirit.

Chawla asked Om*ji*, 'How did you do it?

'*Arey yaar* eat the fruit, don't bother about trees.' Om*ji* could only say that much.

But Chawla had learnt his lesson. He decided to look for a suitable match for Anil without further delay and with renewed vigor.

***

TEN

The window of the Jetlite Air flight to Kochi framed a hazy picture with grey swirls of mist, suffused with afternoon light revealing fleeting glimpses of steely blue sea below. Parvathi sitting in the business class, pointed towards the velvety carpet of brilliant green land flecked with sloping sun-baked roofs as the plane started it's descent slicing though a swathe of thick clouds. Anil could see the tiny rivulet of water beginning its course across the window pane. Another stream joined and soon outside view was obscured by thick sheet of rain.

Anil was traveling to Kochi for the first time and his excitement was infused with nervousness and anticipation in equal measure. Not only the view was enchanting but Parvathi's presence with him for next three days added to his nervousness. As the plane landed and started taxiing to the terminal he could see that the downpour had slowed to a benign drizzle and everything glowed clean and bright.

They took a taxi feeling amused at the driver who was so short he'd have to stand on a brick to kick a duck in the ass. Sitting in the car on way to the hotel Anil wondered at the palm-filled countryside, lush in varying shades of green, air chilled and redolent with the fragrance of fresh earth. The unspoiled tarmac offered a comfortable car ride to the Old

Harbour Hotel in Fort Cochin where they had two deluxe rooms waiting for them.

After more than an hour, negotiating the city center of Ernakulam they entered Fort Cochin and life seemed to slow down all of a sudden. Anil could not fail to notice the quietness of the place broken by the mild chatter of the locals after a days work and the rain stung breeze carrying a strong smell of the sea.

Parvathi pointed towards the gabled, colonial-era bungalows and the narrow winding streets. She explained in brief a bit of history of the place starting from the early traders of Jewish and Christian origin and ending at the British rule with Portuguese and Dutch rule in between.

They were received by the gracious staff of the hotel. As they freshened up in their rooms they looked through the white arched windows overlooking the pristine lawn of the hotel. After thirty minutes Parvathi and Anil were sitting in the Malabar House Bar, five minutes walk from heir hotel sampling wine and prawn 'samosas'.

'So dear, I am in Parvathi's own country now. How do you feel?' Anil asked.

'I am really excited Anil. I am coming here after long and first time alone,' Parvathi replied.

'But you are with me, not alone.'

'I mean without the rest of the family.'

'So what's the agenda for tomorrow?' Anil asked.

'I will tell you later. But let's enjoy this moment. The day hasn't ended,' Parvathi said looking around savoring the ambience.

Parvathi ordered traditional food with Mediterranean twist: shredded duck bathed in spiced coconut cream with fennel and pineapple. They also ordered Kerala style lamb cooked with curry leaves, coconut and shallots.

'This food really tastes good, honey,' Anil said, twirling his tongue.

'Yes it has to be; one doesn't get it in Delhi. I always wanted you to taste it so that you could realize that good food doesn't begin and end with butter-chicken.' Parvathi smiled and teased him.

After a sumptuous meal, Parvathi was ready to hit the sack but Anil suggested they should sit outside their hotel and listen to the sound of sea waves lashing against the shore. As Parvathi sat beside him her head resting on his shoulders, Anil wondered at her beauty and simplicity and thought how mistaken north Indians are about south Indians. He liked the place from the moment he set his foot on the soil of Kochi. Parvathi's company, the somewhat unusual wet weather and its aroma, the quietness of the place and the delicious food banished all misgivings he had about the place.

They felt calm and sleepy and Parvathi suggested that they should call it a day. When Anil tried to kiss her on her lips she brought her palm in between and said, 'No naughty acts before marriage.'

They said bye to each other and instantly hit the bed in their separate rooms.

Next morning Anil woke up to the sound of the rain. He looked at his watch and moaned. It was only 7.30a.m. He called Parvathi's room. As there was no answer, he came out of his room and found her sitting in the lawn enjoying the morning sun.

'How come you're up so early?' Anil asked.

'I usually get up early but I had a bad dream quite early in the morning and woke up.' Parvathi answered.

'What was that?'

'Leave it. It's just a dream.'

'Come on, please tell me,' Anil requested, cupping her face with his hands.

'Ok Baba, if you insist. I dreamt that you were marrying someone else. Your parents had selected a girl from your community and forced you into marrying her. Left all alone, I am running away from you and suddenly a speeding car knocks me down and I am unconscious. When I regain consciousness I find myself on a wheel chair. I am informed I would never be able to walk again. Suddenly I wake up and find it hard to lie down in the bed and come out to sit in the fresh air.'

Anil felt touched. He kissed her and this time she didn't stop him.

'Don't think rubbish, nothing can stop us from marriage. We have to just manage our families. We can marry any time honey, but we don't want to make it painful for our parents. I hope everything shall turn out to be fine. If by any chance things don't work out the way we want, we would still marry. I hope it's clear?' Anil affectionately draped his arms around her.

Parvathi smiled and pressed his hand.

'Let's go and see the Fort after breakfast. I'll join you in forty-five minutes.' She rose and went back to her room.

After breakfast they explored Fort Cochin on foot wandering through lanes and Anil was amused to see endearing names of streets like Lilly Street and Princess Street. They bought few souvenirs and by lunchtime the drizzle had started again and they decided to have an early lunch of spicy shrimp, vegetable thoran and seer fish on banana leaves.

After lunch Anil and Parvathi went to see Mattancherry Palace built in 1555 with its intricate murals that adorn the walls executed in vegetable and mineral dyes.

After a long day Parvathi needed rest and went to her room while Anil decided to have an 'Ayurvedic' massage to soothe his nerves and rejuvenate himself.

Later, at dinner Parvathi reminded Anil that her parents would soon invite him over for a meal at their home. He must try to win them over as it would certainly make things easier. Parvathi apprised him about her mother in particular.

'You know my father and mother met each other here in Fort Cochin. They may ask you about your observations about this place,' Parvathi said.

'Is your mother from Kochi?'

'No. She is from Trivandrum now called Thiruvananthapuram. She had come here on a visit to Fort Kochi. They met on Loafer's Street,' Parvathi explained.

'What a street to meet each other.' Anil burst out laughing.

Parvathi smiled.

'Tell me honestly, which of the two cities your mother likes more, I mean Kochi or Trivandrum?' Anil enquired.

'Kochi. She married early. She practically grew up in Kochi before everyone moved to Delhi. Even now her visits to Kerala means a visit to Kochi not Thiruvananthapuram.'

'That makes it easier I suppose. Otherwise I would have been planning to visit Thiruvananthapuram as well,' Anil quipped.

'Tomorrow I am planning to see your *kathakali* dance,' Anil said helping himself with sips of Munnar tea after a delicious meal.

'I don't dance. What do you mean your *kathakali* dance?' Parvathi puzzled, asked.

'I meant *kathakali* dance of Kerala.'

'Sure we will.' Parvathi looked excited.

Though it was late Anil and Parvathi were not tired. They walked hand in hand on the wet grass outside their hotel.

When the clock tower struck eleven, Anil led Parvathi to her room and looked into her eyes and sensing her readiness, kissed her on the lips as he pushed the door close with his leg. He kissed her lips, face and her neck and they remained in each others arms for long, gasping for breath.

Suddenly, Parvathi slithered away from his embrace and pushed him gently out of her room.

They both had a peaceful sleep that night.

They got up late in the morning. At seven Parvathi called Anil's room and suggested a late breakfast, to which he readily agreed half asleep. They finally met for breakfast at half-past ten.

'As it's our last day here I need to buy few samples of spices before we go for the dance performance,' Anil reminded himself.

They both bought souvenirs, Munnar tea and spices and watched the colorful and recognizable kathakali dance.

'You know in Kathakali we learn the form first. Then through practice life is filled into that form. It's the most refined pantomime dance-drama. It has very old origin.' Parvathi explained before the dance performance began.

Anil was impressed by the elaborate costumes and make up done by the artists. Of all the places, he had seen this dance form in USA as a student when a dance troupe from India had visited New York during Indian Independence Day celebrations. He could not appreciate it as much as he could this time since Parvathi explained to him in hushed voice the intricate expressions of the artists.

Later, he felt a sense of achievement in watching through the entire dance drama. He could now tell his friends in Delhi what it was all about.

'I feel bad our visit is coming to an end so soon,' Anil said.

'How come? I always thought you would miss Delhi after a while. You want to stay more?' Parvathi genuinely surprised by his remark, asked.

'I swear. I never knew Kerala was so beautiful. I haven't seen the whole of it. I have been to Trivandrum once, long time back,' Anil said, and added, 'but this time it has been completely different. I have seen it with the best guide I could ever get.'

'Thanks Anil,' Parvathi said controlling her tears of joy.

Later during dinner of chilli fried crabs, mixed vegetable *avial*, mutton *biryani* and Malabar *porotta*, Parvathi reminded him of their early morning flight to Delhi and the need to pack up and sleep early.

But Anil wanted to enjoy every moment of the quiet, pristine atmosphere in the restaurant, sipped wine and offered to Parvathi also. When she refused he asked her to just taste it for the occasion.

She hesitated and sipped from his half empty glass. He asked her to finish it as he ordered another for himself.

They reached their rooms around midnight savoring every moment of their togetherness as the sea waves lashed the shores and its sound could be heard from distance.

When Parvathi unlocked her room, Anil tapped on her shoulder and as she turned to face him he took her in his arms and kissed her passionately. She responded with equal passion and intensity. They slumped down on the sofa and explored each other with their tongue and fingers.

The sound of thunder and lightening outside broke their embrace as Parvathi tried to free her and whispered to wait till marriage. Anil kissed her and nodded his head. They talked for another thirty minutes and decided that family or no family, they will marry within few months. But before taking the final plunge, they would earnestly try to bring their families together. Also, they would come for their honeymoon to Kochi and stay in the same hotel to complete the incomplete intimate act.

They both kissed each other good night.

Next morning, as their plane took off for Delhi Anil's perception about Kerala had changed and Parvathi had realized and appreciated the qualities she observed in her future husband. They did not talk much, sat with their hands glued together and mind at peace.

***

ELEVEN

Growing frustration with responses on marriage portal tormented Lathika and Nair no end. They were not satisfied with the proposals received, ranging from young men working in Gulf to businessmen, professionals, divorcees, widowers and salaried clerks back home in Kerala.

The outrageous proposal was from a clerk Mr Iyer, working in the state Health Department. Nair found it so funny that he was tempted to read it aloud.

It read, '*In responding to your matrimony in kerala.com I press myself and press myself hoping you will think nicely. I live with my own self in Munnar, the land of hills and tea.*

Your daughter is studied and big in Yemerica while I am son of the soil but I am nice and big five feet, ten inches tall and 5 inches long. I am playing and working hardly and my body is with hardness. I can bowl as fast as Sreesanth. Do you like cricket? If yes you would be afraid of my rapid fire balls.

I am jolly gay and laugh all the time. I respect women and allow them to be on my top. See how nice I am. I don't drink or smoke. I go to gym and pump every dumb belles there.

My pant is full of money and it is always open for your daughter. I live alone so I am taking things in my own hand and if our daughter is marrying me she will have no problem with my pumping dumb belles in gymn.

I press your feet and press you and press you till you bless me as I keep my head between your two leg.

I am very expectant..........'

Lathika raging with anger stopped Nair to read any further. Another response was equally ludicrous. It was from a Malayali working in Gulf. Nair read it silently and feeling disgusted.

'*I am very pleased to introduce myself as Mr Kutty from Kerala, your own land of God. I have two houses in Kochi, one in Ernakulam where my parents live. I am yearning lots and lots of money with my hard work here in Muscat and will keep your daughter very happy and smiling. Let me know if you like me as I am also technical worker your daughter is. I will fall on your feet and will marry when Lord Apayyam is blessing me soon. You will have good grandchildren from me. I don't drink Todi nor I smoke. I like chicken and fish curry. Waiting for your reply and to fly to you soon........'*

Few parents had also responded. Nair deleted their proposal equally fast. He cursed himself for advertising his daughter on internet.

'These stupid people have diarrhea of words and constipation of thoughts.' Nair mumbled.

'Don't bother me with such responses. To me it is as exciting as watching grass grow.' Lathika was terribly disappointed.

Four proposals received from Sreejith from Kozhikode, Achyuth from Calicut, Govindraj from Malappuram and Raghu from Thiruvanthapuram, all software engineers in Kerala looked reasonably good to Nair but the problem was they all had salaries in the range of Rs Four-Five Lakhs per annum where as Parvathi earned Rs Ten Lakhs a year. Earlier Parvathi and Lathika had made their intention known to Nair that the boy's earnings should be more than that of the girl as it might lead to clash of egos and complications in future.

Nair frustrated, turned off his laptop.

****

Parvathi delivered a typed formal letter, signed by her father, inviting Anil and his colleagues Rajesh Talwar and Jacob Thomas for dinner next Saturday at their house.

Parvathi knew that Rajesh and Jacob were out of country and only Anil would come home and that's what she wanted. She informed her parents only on Saturday morning that Anil would be coming alone as the other two were out, leaving no chance for any postponement of dinner.

Anil reached Parvathi's house at 8 pm sharp, to be greeted by Mrs. Bhasin's dog who happily wagged his tail in welcome. Anil picked up the dog in his hands thinking he must impress the dog before he tries to impress its master. It was only when Parvathi who opened the door informed him about its real owner and the hatred and ill will her father possessed for the little creature and its owner that Anil let it go. Parvathi led him to the drawing room and soon left to join her mother.

As Anil waited for her parents, his roving eyes took stock of the room. A women's magazine 'Vanitha' was on the side table along with 'The Hindu' newspaper which he picked up and glanced at the headlines. The wait didn't last long as the familiar figure of Mr. Nair emerged from the side door.

As Anil rose to say 'namastey' he didn't fail to notice that Nair was dressed informally in a *lungi*, a three yard piece of cloth to cover his modesty and a shirt, hanging out. He could not stop his mind thinking why scientific research has not been able to uncover the secret of how this dress manages to stay in place, a sartorial miracle itself. The men could do anything in their lungis, from playing football to driving bikes without the knot loosening.

'Good evening Anil, how do you do? We are happy you accepted our invitation. Parvathi speaks very high of you. We also remember your party during Onam few days back, I say.' Nair made himself comfortable on the sofa opposite him.

'I am fine sir, thanks. It was because of special persons like you, the Onam celebration party became lively.' Anil had not expected Nair would remember it after so many days.

Soon they were joined by Lathika and Parvathi. Lathika reminded him about her promise to cook Kerala cuisine for everyone and expressed disappointment at the absence of his colleagues. Anil expressed regret that his friends could not come as they were out of the country, and hoped the secret would never come out.

'Parvathi told us that you were in *Yemerica* earlier. My two cousins are in *Yemerica* working in the health industry. When did you come to Delhi?' Lathika asked.

'Sorry, where is *Yemerica*?' Anil muttered looking at Parvathi a bit puzzled.

Parvathi smiled and Anil understood it was the Kerala accent and he sheepishly nodded.

'Oh, I came home last year. My parents live here in Delhi.'

'Are they in service?' Nair asked.

'No, they have a business of their own. We have few sari shops in and around old parts of Delhi. It's an old family business.'

'You didn't find business attractive enough?' Lathika asked.

'As a matter of fact I like salaried job. It has fewer tensions in life. It may not be very rewarding monetarily but it provides a regulated life.' Anil admitted and asked, 'how do you feel working for a salary these thirty years?'

'I share your belief Anil. Salaried life is better and more organized. But my wife does not share my belief, I say,' Nair replied.

Anil realized he had to tread carefully as the Nair's were divided on this issue.

He tried to change the topic but Lathika intervened, 'Business provides more opportunities and one is better off financially. Moreover, a business-man can be master of his own time. Mr. Nair has given the best part of his life to Government, yet he could not become a Joint secretary or a *yedditional* (additional) Secretary here as he belongs to Central Secretariat Service. He is still a Director. He has been only working for his IAS bosses all these years. Had he been in business he would have risen higher. Moreover, we could have had opportunities to be nearer to Kerala. His cousins who are in 'gelff' (Gulf) are doing extremely fine.'

Anil realized it was Lathika who called the shots in the family as Nair sat still like a lame duck listening to her wife's anguish. He considered it prudent to avoid being sucked into a family debate.

The conversation shifted to Kerala. Nair and Lathika told Anil about the natural beauty of Kerala as Parvathi brought four small cups of hot Lipton tea on a tray and offered to Anil and her parents and joined them listening attentively to their conversation.

'I agree. Among all places I have visited in India I like Kerala the most,' Anil said. 'Its greenery, quietness, cuisine and people fascinate me. Mountains of bananas, yards of jasmine, rows of glass bangles and shimmering satin ribbons in rainbow hues, trinkets and toys enchant me during festival times. I feel quite at peace with myself.' Anil was surprised the way he could describe Kerala. He remembered the adjectives used in the books on Kerala.

'Do you visit Kerala often?' asked Lathika.

'I keep going to Kerala for company work.' Anil purposely stated to show his interest in Kerala.

'Really? I am surprised,' Lathika said. 'Although Keralites these days dislike what's become of Kerala today, very seldom will you find a Keralite who can resist the temptation to go home especially when the festivals beckon.'

'Can I offer you a drink? I prefer whiskey.' Nair sitting silent for some time asked all of a sudden.

'I can take whiskey.' Anil replied, thinking this would allow him to stay and talk long and provide him an opportunity to find more about their likes and dislikes.

As Nair went inside to arrange drinks, Lathika resumed.

'See, we are destroying Kerala. Like all other places we have cut and slashed, dug and hewed, ravaged and wrecked and dirtied and littered.'

'How?' asked Anil.

'The Forest department cut the trees. The electricity people built dams and drowned the remaining trees. We have expanded and diversified the onslaught in our own way. We could not do much to moon and stars or the sunset and sunrise so they are the same. Air quality has taken a beating.' Lathika complained.

Nair came back with two glasses of whiskey and offered one to Anil.

Anil said, 'but still from some hills and mountains you can get good view. Forests have lot of trees and.....'

'That's because the Forest Department find it hard to reach. Nor can you.' Nair intervened.

Nair further said, 'you know we Malayalis strongly believe that there is nothing that succeeds like success. If one house-boat succeeds there'll soon appear more of them and so is the case with Ayurveda resorts. They mushroom like anything. I would not be surprised if soon the pure backwaters, hills, estates and beaches are taken over and ravaged by the tourism industry, I say.'

Anil thought about this and appreciated what Nair said. This would be true of many places. He felt Nair was a thinking type person with an analytical bent of mind. Then he thought and started visualizing how the conversation between his Dad and Nair would take place. But Whiskey didn't help his thinking process.

Lathika and Parvathi exchanged glances and they got up to set the table for dinner. Nair offered Anil another peg of whiskey and their conversation about changes taking place in Kerala continued.

At the dinner table Anil found a lavish spread of Kerala cuisine ranging from fish curry, *avial*, mutton *biryani*, *kootu*-curry, *sambhar*, *porottas* and *payasam*, a rich milky delicacy with vermicelli and rice for dessert. Anil felt embarrassed looking at the lavish dinner prepared for him and thinking about his colleague's absence tonight. Mrs. Nair and Parvathi had worked all day to produce this delectable cuisine. He couldn't stop himself from eating more than he usually had for dinner. 'If Parvathi cooked as well as her mother, he would gain more weight in a year than he gained in five years,' he thought.

His random thoughts were broken when Lathika asked him, 'Are there nice looking eligible Malayali bachelors in your company Anil?'

'Yes there are a couple of them. I think you had met them at the Onam party. May I ask why?' Anil asked a bit alarmed at the suddenness of the question.

'We are looking for a match for our Parvathi.' Nair helped himself with a spoon of payasam.

Anil who was eating his dessert suddenly felt choked and coughed, the spoon falling on the plate. Parvathi helped him with another spoon. As he looked at Parvathi to say thanks, he saw her smiling.

Anil feeling better and composed, asked Nair who was sitting next to him, 'But sir, why only a Malayali boy, there are many others I know.'

'Lathika doesn't trust boys and their families from north. It's ironical that we have lived here for last thirty years and could not place our trust in anyone, I say.' Nair replied looking at his wife who nodded.

'But Sir, don't you think a region or a community shouldn't be blamed in general? I mean, if by any chance your experience in Delhi has not been good with people, would it necessarily mean all Delhites are untrustworthy?' Anil confronted them.

'You are right. I do not believe in this as much as my wife does. There are good and bad people everywhere. We have plenty of bad characters in our state of Kerala, I say.' Nair answered, not liking his guest feel embarrassed.

Lathika spoke, 'My experience is limited to my own domestic life. All my servants from Delhi ditched me. Two of them committed theft in our own house. Mr Nair leads an official life every day and he doesn't completely agree with my views about Delhites. I may be wrong. For example you are also a boy from north and you are a real gem Anil. Parvathi speaks very high of you. We have met your friends at the Onam party. They all seemed nice to us. We want a Malayali boy from Kerala not because of a dearth of decent, responsible boys here. We want it because we feel the families in Delhi find it difficult to accept a girl from south. I understand there are cultural differences but not insurmountable ones.'

Encouraged by Mrs. Nair's words, Anil said, 'These days family outlook has undergone change Aunti*ji*. The joint family system is breaking down fast. Parents do not interfere as much in the lives of children as they used to do earlier. Liberalism is the essence of family life now. There are even differences between two families of Delhi. A business family may have different social and cultural pattern of life than a family of salary earners. I feel, in marriage, compatibility between two persons is more important than their family background.'

Parvathi who had hardly spoken during the entire evening said, 'Any girl today would like to marry someone who she can connect to easily. More important than family background is the similarity of intellect and outlook. Families offer no guarantee that marriage will stand the test of future.'

Nair said, 'I agree with Parvathi. Times have changed. A daughter of my north Indian colleague who is in Delhi married a young handsome boy from a business family of Delhi. In six months they separated. Now she is dating a Tamil boy, son of another colleague of mine. I think more than region or community, it's the family sub-culture which is important, I say.'

Anil suddenly realized that he should counter this argument vehemently as it may apply to his case.

He said, 'Sir, I have seen many marriages within business families or service class families breaking up despite similar family sub-culture. Therefore, I feel it has not as much to do with family occupation than similarities between two individuals.'

Lathika who was listening for a while remarked, 'I agree Anil, but in case of marital discord and disputes the families do help each other if they share identical interests. In India marriages are not yet purely an individual alliance. It's a family institution.'

'I do agree it's an institution and the family has an important role to play. All I am saying is that considerations of region, caste or family occupations are as important in Delhi as they are in Tamilnadu, Andhra, Punjab or Kerala. These considerations by themselves do not protect or demolish the matrimonial edifice. What can protect a marriage from falling apart is compatibility between two individuals otherwise nothing can save it.' Anil expounded as everyone listened to him.

Parvathi encouraged, said, 'I can't think of sticking to someone if he doesn't like me or I don't like him even if his family loves and adores me.'

Nair suggested they move back to the drawing room area for further discussion on this subject and everyone agreed.

It seemed Lathika's turn to speak and she finally made the evening for Anil by saying, 'you are right Anil, times have changed. But find me a good boy for Parvathi, as understanding and intelligent as you are, or maybe even better. She is our only child. But the boy's family should accept her willfully and with open arms.'

Nair who fixed red wine for himself offered Anil who readily accepted, wishing to prolong the conversation.

Nair said, 'Our Parvathi is very dear to us. We trust her judgment. All we want is a decent family which accepts her without reservations and the boy should be acceptable to her and to us. I agree with you that difference of caste, region or culture, though important should not override individual preferences and choice, I say.'

Anil knew he had won his battle. Mr. & Mrs. Nair liked him. He had to make his own parents approve his choice of a wife now.

His thoughts were broken as Lathika said, 'Have you chosen someone to marry? Or still looking out?' The suddenness of the question and its personal nature shook Anil out of his reverie.

Anil composed his thoughts and not willing to forego any opportunity replied, 'I do have a couple of girls in mind, but so far could not muster enough courage to ask them about marriage. They belong to family of Government Officers not business men like my parents. One of them is a south Indian. So, you can say I am free and available at present.'

As he said this, he looked at Parvathi from the corner of his eyes and saw her make considerable efforts to contain her laughter.

Nair said, 'you must tell them your feelings and let things take their own course. As you said earlier, the comfort level of two individuals who have to marry should be the deciding factor I say.' Lathika nodded in agreement.

Anil already elated by the progress so far could not hide his excitement and said, 'I will straightaway mention to one of the two girls tomorrow and see how it goes.'

As Anil was about to leave, he presented a packet wrapped in a gift box to Lathika. She looked at her husband who asked Anil what it was. Anil mentioned about his recent trip to Kochi and said, 'though it is like carrying coal back to Newcastle this packet contains a souvenir, Munnar tea and some spices I bought from Kerala.' Mr and Mrs. Nair were touched. They thanked him and asked Parvathi to walk him up to his car.

Before leaving, Anil asked Parvathi what kind of impression her parents might be having about him. She replied that he had won his semifinal match and she has to win her semi-final to be in the finals.

'And who will win the final match?'

'Do I have to tell you, it will be a draw? Both have to be joint winners for the title.' Parvathi replied and waved at him as Anil started the car and humming a Hindi movie song left.

***

TWELVE

Chawla Bhai had not recovered fully from the impact Angad Singh episode created in his psyche. The image of Angad Singh's son and his gun trotting men tormented him during sleep. Even whiskey was not a panacea after a day's hard work as his mind always conjured up images of Angad Singh and his criminal gang. He shared his concerns with Ritu and how Omji managed to get him off the hook. Ritu agreed with him that a suitable match be found for Anil as early as possible. Chawla Bhai informed his brothers and relatives to look for a suitable alliance and Ritu sought help from her parents, relatives and close friends.

An eligible, rich, handsome bachelor in Indian society can retain his bachelorhood only with considerable amount of luck and fortitude. The moment relatives were invited to come forward with offers, proposals did not come like drizzle but started pouring in with thunder and lightening.

Long forgotten friends suddenly announced their daughter's candidature and lofty pecuniary promises were made. Close relatives started paying regular visits with proposals of girls ranging from almost half the height of

Anil to twice his weight. At times it appeared to Ritu and Chawla Bhai as if Anil was put up for a distress sale.

'How can people come to us with such ridiculous offers?' Ritu protested as Chawla Bhai's friend from school came up with his daughter's profile. His daughter had failed twice in Class 12th, gave up studies and weighed seventy-five kilos. He had the audacity to suggest her hand in marriage to Anil who had his higher education in America and worked for a Multinational company and weighed only seventy kilos.

Another proposal came from the family of Chawla Bhai's brother's wife. The girl was a divorcee but her father was willing to spend five Crores for her wedding.

At Gymkhana, Omji and Chawla could never sit and drink in peace any more. Frustrated, Chawla announced that Anil has finally found someone and there was no need to come up with offers any further.

So Ritu and Chawla Bhai decided to stop this whole exercise for the time being and concentrate on responses from matrimonial advertisement already received through mail.

'From now onwards we would meet one or two parents and girls everyday without letting anyone know about it.' Ritu told Chawla Bhai and he agreed instantaneously.

The search yielded positive results and they short listed three Punjabi business families from south and central Delhi.

Even after considerable persuasion and pleadings Anil refused to meet the girls or their parents. Ritu, alarmed at her son's intransigence suggested Chawla Bhai to have a chat with Anil and find out his inclination. Chawla Bhai asked Anil to accompany him to Agra for a short trip. He planned to fathom his son's feelings on the subject during this trip.

'Anil I am not growing any younger. I and your mother wish that you should also settle down soon. We did try to find a suitable girl for you but perhaps couldn't come up with the right offer. Do you have anyone in mind or you don't want to marry at present?' Chawla asked him as they sat comfortably in the back seat of their Mercedes driving towards Agra.

'Papa I don't have anyone particular in my mind. But I am quite sure I can only be happy with that person who is mentally, culturally and intellectually compatible with me. If I find someone I will let you know. Meanwhile you and Mom can continue to look for a suitable alliance.' Anil threw the bait.

'But we short-listed few good proposals from Punjabi families and you turned them down.' Chawla looked at his face.

'Because I felt that while doing so you were guided by caste, community and business concerns. I went through the profiles of the girls you and Mom selected and found out that the girls were not suitable for me. Two were simply graduates with English Literature and History and one was a lawyer by profession. I did not have to meet them to know that. I am a technical person and I had told Mom earlier I would prefer a working girl with same technical background as mine,' Anil explained. 'Why do you limit your choice within Punjabi families or only business families? Three girls you short-listed for me had nothing common with me. All three were from rich, high social standing Punjabi families. But not my type, that's why I turned them down.'

Chawla Bhai didn't like his son to be so choosy about marriage proposals.

'I really fail to understand why your generation is so much after compatibility, matching nature and qualifications of a girl? Look, Amit married Lovely and is happy with her. I did not know your mother before marriage and she adjusted herself in the family. In my time, the adjustment and compatibility developed after marriage. A successful marriage requires falling in love many times, always with the same person.'

Anil laughed at his one liner and asked, 'But Papa, how can one make a marriage work these days? It's not easy.'

'Easy my son easy, tell your wife that she looks pretty even if she looks like a truck.' Chawla quipped. 'A man has to manage his wife. The other night, your mother and I were going out. She sat there and put on eyebrow pencil, eye shadow, eyeliner, eyelashes, mascara, toner, blush and lipstick, then turned to me and enquired, does this look natural? I had to say yes, quite natural.'

Anil laughed at his father's sense of humour.

"Isn't it good if both husband and wife share common interests and both like the same stuff?' Anil asked.

'True. You've got to find somebody who likes the same stuff. Like, if you like sports, she should like it that you like sports, and she should keep the whiskey and chicken coming.' Chawla said poker faced as Anil laughed once again.

'How did you look for a girl in your days?' Anil asked, enjoying this conversation.

'We looked for good families. *Khata-pita ghar ho*. The girl should know how to run a house, look after her family and the elders so that men could work outside with peace. The role of a wife was very well defined. That's why there were hardly any divorces.' Chawla explained. 'But why don't you realize that family background is also very important?' Chawla asked.

'Yes it is. Equally important are the qualities of the girl. Why do we have to run after money and social prestige all the time? Why can't we have a beautiful, well qualified and simple girl with etiquette who is compatible with me and who would also respect my family and elders? Even if she is not from a high status family of Delhi but from a salaried or middle class, how does it affect us? My way of thinking is different Papa. I consider it more as a human alliance than an alliance of business interests or social position. Ask Mom to find out for me someone who she likes, you also like, but without the mandatory trappings of social standing, business background, caste or regional considerations. I should also find her compatible. In case I find someone, allow me to suggest her name to you.' Anil elaborated, making his intentions and argument very clear.

'You seem to be right. We never thought it this way. You have reduced my stress Anil. I would like to go along with your views. They make sense to me.' Chawla Bhai thought there is no point trying to convince his son.

Anil feeling relieved continued, 'Papa, God has been kind to us. We don't require money through marriage alliances. We have our own social standing. My career is on the right track. If I marry someone who is not Punjabi and very rich but educated, sincere and respectful it would help me and our family. I have no problem with her being a Punjabi and very rich. All I want is that undue premium should not be put upon her being a Punjabi and rich with high social standing.' Anil added.

'I agree,' Chawla said and dozed off.

On return from Agra, Chawla told Ritu about his conversation with Anil. She didn't say anything but Chawla sensed her reluctance to agree with Anil's views on the issue.

****

Anil met Parvathi in the coffee shop at Hyatt Hotel. He told her that the ground work had already been done and she could look forward to bumping into his mother and take things forward from there. But the question which weighed on their minds now was how to organize a meeting between Parvathi and Ritu.

It was Anil who found a way out. He planned to inform Parvathi about his mother's schedule and she would try to be there at the same time and place. He had a vague idea that his mother was supposed to go to her beauty parlor in a day or two. She usually went every weekend after taking appointment through Lovely, her daughter-in-law. Lovely would tell him about the next appointment.

It happened exactly as he had imagined. Ritu had booked an appointment for next Friday at three pm. Parvathi booked for herself.

'Hi, I think we have met. I am Ritu. Ritu Chawla.' Ritu spotted Parvathi sitting in blue faded jeans and pink top having her hair trimmed while reading a magazine.

'Oh! Yes Madam..... Who doesn't know you? I am Parvathi. I was with you at Habitat for the fashion show,' Parvathi said, feigning surprise on seeing her and added, 'You look great Ma'am. I could not recognize you. You look even younger than last time I met you.'

'Don't flatter me Parvathi. I am two months older than last time you saw me. In fact you look ravishing. I didn't know you come to this parlor.' Ritu pleased with her remark said.

While Ritu went through a facial massage, Parvathi had her hair trimmed. They both chatted in between. Ritu complained that Parvathi didn't care to contact her after the fashion show. Parvathi lied that she called once and finding her out of Delhi, left no message.

Ritu showed off saying she was away on foreign tour and had just come back, while thinking that it was quite possible that Parvathi might have called when she had gone to visit her relatives in Bhatinda, Punjab.

After the visit to the parlor, Ritu suggested coffee at Hotel Intercontinental nearby.

As they sat in the coffee shop, Ritu enquired about the latest in the fashion industry. Parvathi was not prepared but could satisfy her reasonably well through her own knowledge perfunctorily gained through newspapers and journals.

'You know after the fashion show Rekha and you organized here, I went to attend the Lakme fashion week in Mumbai. Later Rita Beri invited me to Paris for her show.' Ritu told Parvathi.

'Great. I seem to have read about your presence in Mumbai and Paris. Maybe I saw your photo in the press as well. How I wish to see a show like that.' Parvathi said and realized immediately that she had made a mistake saying this.

Ritu eyed her suspiciously and wondered how Parvathi could read it in the press as she herself never attended the Mumbai event or went to Paris.

'Who all are in your family Parvathi?' Ritu asked during their talk.

'I am the only child of my parents. We are from Kerala and have lived in Delhi for last thirty years. My father is a senior officer with Government of India and mother used to teach earlier but is a housewife now.' She told her.

'If I remember correctly you had mentioned that you work in the same Company where my son Anil works. Isn't it?' Ritu asked.

Parvathi thought about it trying to remember where she had mentioned it. Then she realized that Ritu had introduced her son Anil to her after the show in Habitat.

'Yes Ma'am. It's a big Company and I couldn't meet him after the event.'

'Where did you have your education Parvathi?'

'I studied in Delhi and later in US,' Parvathi answered.

'It's a strange coincidence. My son also studied in Delhi and America.'

Parvathi kept silent. Ritu studied her face thinking who she resembles. Suddenly it occurred to her that her face resembles Vidya Balan, a Bollywood actress.

'Are you related to Vidya Balan an actress in Mumbai who is originally from Kerala?' Ritu asked.

'No Ma'am, I am not. Though born in Kerala, Vidya Balan is a Tamil Iyer girl, daughter of Mr. P.R.Balan, Vice President of Etc Channel. I like her acting,' Parvathi gleefully answered.

'How do you know all that?'

'Because this is not the first time I have been suspected of having some link with her. Perhaps my face resembles her.' Parvathi blushed.

'How is your friend Rekha doing?'

'She is doing fine. She is working for her next fashion show in Chandigarh after three months or so. It's a very fashion conscious city. I think it should turn out to be a gala event.' Parvathi threw her bait.

'Great. Why don't you come home for a meal with us? You will see our home and meet our family.' Ritu was excited by the casual mention of fashion show in Chandigarh thinking her relatives from Punjab could also attend the show this time.

'Whenever you say Ma'am, it'll be my privilege.' Parvathi was waiting for this opportunity.

'What about lunch day after tomorrow? It's a Sunday and everyone will be home. I can send the car to your address for pickup.' Ritu offered.

'Thanks Ma'am. I'll reach your home. Give me the address.'

'I must rush now. I have a party to attend at eight tonight. Everyone who is someone in Delhi is going to be present and they are voting for different categories of women for the year 2008,' Ritu said looking at her watch.

Ritu handed her visiting card, called for the bill and felt pleased with the meeting with the Vidya Balan look-alike girl who had invited her as a Chief Guest in a fashion show for the first and last time so far.

Parvathi's first call from her mobile went to Anil who sounded happy and asked her to see him after few hours to plan for the upcoming lunch. They agreed to meet in Taj Palace at seven pm.

Anil told Parvathi in detail about his father, Lovely and his elder brother Amit. Parvathi had already heard a lot about Ritu.

Both waited with nervous anticipation for the important meeting to take place on Sunday.

***

THIRTEEN

'Omji, times have changed. Business families should not send their children for higher studies and never to countries like America where they are spoiled.' Chawla Bhai complained after downing a couple of whiskey pegs. Then he narrated his entire conversation with Anil.

'I agree. I am so happy I did not send my son or daughter to England or America. They would have refused to handle family business. We had started our life from scratch after migrating in 1947. Now we find our children consider it beneath their dignity to manage family run shops or marry girls within their own community. You did the right thing Chawla by not sending your eldest son Amit to England. At least he is managing your business and his wife Lovely though from a transporter family of Azadpur looks after your home.' Om*ji* commiserated with him.

'Omji what can I do? I have tried to reason with Anil but his arguments are somewhat convincing and I fail to counter them. I told him that our business, social circle and standing grows through matrimonial alliances but he stubbornly disagrees with my views and thinks that compatibility and similarity of outlook between husband and wife override all other considerations. He has a point. After all he has to marry and live with his wife. I wish he had not been thinking so logically and independently.'

'Why couldn't you or Ritu *bhabhi* find a girl who could address Anil's concerns as well as your own?'

'I tried. You know Ritu as much as I do. She would prefer a girl who would flatter and compliment her for her taste and looks all the time. She would like a daughter-in-law who can accompany her to parlors, fashion shows, social gatherings and parties and through her she could bask in the reflected glory.' Chawla Bhai enjoying his fourth peg and taking a bite from his plate of butter-chicken, added.

'What about relatives and other friends, you didn't ask any of them for advice?'

'Of course, I did. They came up with stupid proposals, not worthy enough for consideration. *khote hain*.' Chawla retorted.

'I have an idea. Ask Anil to find a girl himself. In case you and Ritu Bhabhi like her and her family, its fine. Otherwise tell Anil we don't like her and her family, give solid reasons for doing so, and ask him to find another. This way, either your problem would be solved or Anil would become so fed up with his quest for a suitable girl that he would yield and then you can decide in favor of a suitable family and girl.' Om*ji*, as usual, had a solution for everything under the sky.

Chawla pondered and could not dig any hole in this suggestion.

'But how do I tackle Ritu? She never liked Amit's wife Lovely. So far Ritu has kept mum and refrained from running her down as Lovely's family is in the league of big transporters of Delhi. But see how well Lovely looks after the entire household, while her mother-in-law flits from one social party to another. I am afraid, she may quickly approve Anil's wrong choice and I would be left high and dry. Or if I choose someone right for Anil, she may side with Anil and out rightly reject her.' Chawla grumbled.

'Chawla Bhai your family is quite complicated and they fly in all directions.' Omji confused, called the waiter and asked for another drink. 'See Bhabhi and all your children think different. Either you go along with any one of them or take *sanyaas* from life leaving everything to Amit and Anil.' He added.

'You are no good friend yaar. Is this your advice?' Chawla visibly hurt, asked.

'What can I say? There are no ready tailor made solutions for your problems. If you want to impose your own thoughts and perceptions on your wife and children who have moved in different directions, it's not going to help things either. No US returned son is going to sit in a saree shop selling sarees all day or would select a bride who would only run the household and prepare chicken and *patiala* whiskey pegs for her husband and good for nothing in-laws. I have adjusted to my life. I didn't commit the same mistake which you did. We as a community pretend and want to show off to the world outside but in our hearts we are typical old fashioned confused Punjabi male chauvinists and don't know what actually we want. Chawla, you seem to be trapped in a phase of social and cultural change.'

'You have a point Om*ji*. But how can you talk such sense after so many whiskey pegs?' Chawla was genuinely surprised.

'I lose my inhibition and speak honestly. That's all,' Om*ji* said. He added, 'this is the difference between Old Delhi and New Delhi. We in Old Delhi are firmly rooted to our culture and old habits while our Punjabi friends in South Delhi have moved ahead from traditional business and social circles to modern business processes and contemporary social circles. We have no right to pass a judgment sitting on a high pedestal of a moral and ethical umpire. We started our family and business interests when Chandni Chowk and Daryaganj were the most coveted and plush localities in the city. Now they are not. You know Ritu Bhabhi's father had a small restaurant in Daryaganj. I am not sure whether it would even qualify to be a restaurant. Then he moved south and opened few more in New Delhi and he and his children are happy looking after their modern family businesses in New Delhi. They moved with times. You could only extend up-to Karolbagh and C.P. physically but not mentally or socially.' Omji expounded.

'Om*ji*, everyone is dishing out arguments these days which I find hard to counter. I never knew you also have views on this subject. But what you say does make sense. Let's see what Anil does. I'll tell him to look for a suitable girl himself. I would see how things take shape later.' Chawla Bhai gulped his drink and thought of going home as his mind was muddled.

'Have one more for the road.' Om*ji* said. He pointed to the waiter passing by, and tapping Chawla's thighs continued, 'Chawla Bhai, be happy and lead your life and let others live their own. We have established our business and children. Now it's up to them to take it further. A time may come when Amit's children may not like to run your shops. Does that mean Amit should not provide them with good education? Time changes and so does everything. I did not send my children abroad but I really feel guilt in my heart. Because of my narrow selfish interest I played with their life. I see how they fail to mix up with their cousins in South Delhi who consider them small timers. Our children suffer from an inferiority complex. Their cousins are well educated, handling modern businesses, factories or working in MNC's. My sons avoid being part of the elite in the city. How many people know Amit? But a lot more know Anil. If he thinks he needs a girl with whom he can lead a normal and modern life, what's the harm? At least for the sake of our children we should stop being selfish.'

Chawla thought about it and felt a difference between Amit and Anil, his two sons.

'Om*ji* I never thought about all this. You seem to have a point here.'

'Chawla, never interfere too much in the lives of children. Don't mess up their lives by trying to make them see the world through your own eyes. We are not educated, but we both have seen the world. You don't have a daughter but I have one. I know more than half of divorces in the city of Delhi take place because of interference of mothers in the lives of their daughters. The minds of daughters are influenced and prejudiced by constant hammering received from their mothers. They start viewing everything from their mother's perspective. And when things go wrong mothers shift the entire blame on others. They can't blame themselves nor do they find it easy to blame their own daughters. This further aggravates the problem.

'My daughter Dolly was on the brink of a divorce. It's just my good luck and the understanding nature of my son-in-law which saved the day for me. My wife would leave no stone unturned to poke her nose in our daughter's life and vitiate the family atmosphere at her daughter's home. And on top of that your bhabhi would never realize her folly. This would further aggravate the family situation at my son-in-law's home.'

Already drunk and having completely lost his inhibitions, Omji broke down and started sobbing.

It had become embarrassing for Chawla. He wiped Om*ji*'s tears and escorted him to his chauffer driven car and stepped towards his own.

Like earlier, Om*ji* had solved Chawla's problem. Though tipsy, he could clearly see what his future course of action should be.

On way home Chawla Bhai kept thinking about what Omji said. He decided he would share it with Ritu.

He lay on his bed, couldn't sleep, watched TV and waited for Ritu to come home from her party. After a while Chawla dozed off.

Ritu had a highly successful party in which she was declared the winner for the year 2008 award for the most well dressed women in her club. Congratulations had flowed in and as usual she nodded condescendingly and accepted her moments of triumph. She wanted to tell Chawla Bhai her accomplishment as soon as possible.

When Ritu entered the bedroom past midnight she found the TV on. She switched it off, changed into her night dress and retired to bed quietly not wanting to wake up Chawla.

After a while she became aware that her husband was touching her in a most unusual manner. He started by running his hand across her shoulders and the small of her back. His hands very lightly touched her breasts.

Then he proceeded to run his hand gently down her side, sliding his hand over her stomach, and then down the other side to a point below her waist. He continued on gently feeling her hips till his hands ran further down the outside of her thighs.

Ritu wondered what had happened to her husband, though she became aroused and squirmed a little to better position herself. Then it stopped all of a sudden and she could feel her husband roll over to his side of the bed.

She asked him, 'what happened dear? Why have you stopped?'

Chawla Bhai, wide awake now touched her arm and said endearingly, 'nothing my *titli*, I found the remote of the TV I had been looking for.'

Ritu abruptly pushed his hand resting on her arm, rolled over and went to sleep. Chawla Bhai thought it prudent to talk next morning.

He kept on thinking about what Omji said and could sleep only very late.

In the morning Ritu informed Chawla, Amit, Anil and Lovely that she has been adjudged the best dressed woman of the year 2008 and will have Parvathi for Lunch on Sunday. Everyone congratulated her. But it was Anil who was most expressive in his comments. He said, 'Mom, I knew it. No one in Delhi can score points over you when it comes to dress sense. I saw in Habitat the other day how even fashion industry girls swoon over you when it comes to elegance and dress sense.'

Mention of Habitat and the fashion show reminded Ritu that Parvathi is a colleague of Anil. She said, 'You have reminded me at the right time. You must stay home for lunch on Sunday. You remember Parvathi, the one who gave speech and organized the event at Habitat, she is coming over.'

'But Mom I had planned to go to a movie with Rajesh.' Anil pretended to protest.

'No way, you can go some other day.'

'Ok I will stay back.' Anil relented.

Chawla Bhai tried to excuse himself by saying that he might have to go to his brother Ramesh's place in Karolbagh. But Ritu was in no mood to listen today. She was not yet out of her evening party winning hangover. She agreed to accompany him to his brother's place after lunch. Chawla Bhai made no further excuses.

Later, Chawla told Ritu briefly what Om*ji* had said though he found Ritu mentally preoccupied. He told Anil that he should start looking for a suitable girl for himself. Anil perplexed by the suddenness of his father's advice, nodded nonchalantly as he had already selected his girl.

***

FOURTEEN

Parvathi arrived ten minutes before one and was immediately ushered into the drawing room. Few minutes later, she was with Ritu and Sunil Chawla and exchanging pleasantries. Lovely and Amit joined in and Anil was the last to walk in, shook hands with Parvathi and welcomed her at his residence.

'Hi, it's a shame we hardly get to see each other at the work place,' Anil said loudly to make himself heard in the room. Looking towards Ritu he said, 'It's so nice Mom to invite Parvathi for lunch. At least I can tell my friends in office that I do socialize. Everyone thinks my life revolves around work only.' He added, 'Thanks for coming Parvathi.'

'Parvathi didn't know that you would be around. She didn't even remember that I am your mother when I bumped into her in the parlor. In fact I invited her to meet all of you over lunch. I am so happy at least we all are together for lunch. Otherwise on Sundays it's just me and your Papa at home.' Ritu said in a tone of complaint.

Chawla Bhai thought how correct his wife Ritu was about their children. On holidays he missed their presence badly. He didn't remember when the whole family had lunch together last.

'Parvathi, do your parents miss you as much as we miss our children on holidays?' Chawla asked. 'In our home, holidays are worse than working days. At least on working days my daughter in law Lovely is with us but on Sundays Amit and Lovely come home by the time we are going to sleep. Anil is busy with friends,' he added.

'Uncle, on Sundays I am usually at home except when I go to movie with a friend. I help my Papa and Mummy,' Parvathi answered.

'How nice, I wish I had a daughter like you,' Chawla moaned.

Ritu talked to Parvathi about her family as Chawla Bhai listened. Lovely went to the kitchen to get soft drinks. Amit and Anil talked about cricket.

'I am told you were in US for higher studies and have come home recently.' Amit tried to start a polite conversation as Lovely served cold drinks.

Parvathi briefly told him about her studies in America when Lovely interrupted her, 'Mom was so happy after coming from your fashion show. She was on top of the world. She still remembers it and says it was the best show she had ever been to.'

Ritu looked at Lovely and gave her a stern look. She didn't like to be exposed like this. All along Ritu had been telling others that she had been attending fashion shows in Paris and Mumbai and now her daughter in law had spilled the beans. Ritu felt highly embarrassed and thought gold plating doesn't turn a coarse metal into gold.

Lovely couldn't understand the meaning of Ritu's cold stare and stern face. She further said, 'Mom is looking forward to your next show. This time Parvathi, don't forget to invite me and Amit.'

Ritu flinched. She never wanted Parvathi to know that she was actually looking forward to the next show. She felt helpless as her daughter in law continued uncovering her.

'Of course it will be our pleasure to have all of you there for the next show, though I am not directly involved in this. In fact my friend Rekha had organized the last show and I only helped her and suggested that she should call Auntie and Uncle and their friends for the show. I had heard a lot about Auntie doing much for social causes in Delhi. I really admire her for her grace, dress sense and the way she carries herself. And true to herself she donated a decent sum for the Fashion Institute.' Parvathi not letting go any opportunity to praise Ritu, explained to Lovely.

Chawla Bhai flinched remembering the donation. But Ritu's mood, after Lovely's faux-paus returned to normal as she crossed her legs and sat upright, suddenly beaming with a feeling of glory and self-pleasure.

'It was a small gesture. But I am sure Rekha's next show is going to be a bigger hit. You mentioned about Chandigarh as the next venue,' Ritu said. Then turning towards Chawla she added, 'Sunil tell all your clients, relatives and friends to make the show a success and Parvathi don't bother, I shall be there to assist you.' Ritu invited herself.

Chawla asked Parvathi about her parents and on being informed that her father was a bureaucrat and a Keralite suddenly lost interest in her.

'So your parents must be looking forward to going back to Kerala after retirement. I have been to Kerala once. I liked Kovalam Beach. How do you feel thinking about returning to your home land,' Chawla asked.

'We are definitely not going back to Kerala so haven't thought about our return. We have lived in Delhi for thirty years and it's our second home now,' Parvathi replied.

'But won't your family miss their ancestral place?'

'Yes they do even now but not to the extent that they would migrate after Papa's retirement. Had it been so, my father would have left his job long back and returned to Kerala. He likes his job and his company of Civil Service officers. He loves Kerala, but his friends and associates are here in Delhi. He is an intellectual and prefers stimulating company rather just the company of relatives and kinsmen from his native place.' Parvathi offered her explanation with conviction.

'That's nice to hear. I thought people go to far-off places to earn money and make a career and return at the first opportunity. Keralites go to Gulf countries to earn money and come back as soon as they become rich.' Chawla Bhai innocently embarrassed his entire family.

'True. And so are Sikhs and Punjabis working as Cab Drivers in New York, Seattle, Vancouver and other places. My father doesn't need to make money as he has enough to last few generations. He didn't come to Delhi to earn money but for his career which gave him satisfaction. It's only that Keralites or South Indians in general, don't show off as some people in North India do,' Parvathi replied tersely. 'My father is happy with his life here which is peaceful and intellectually stimulating for him. He does miss Kerala cuisine, culture and the festivals there. And to take care of that, he often goes home and spends time with his folks,' she added.

Anil could sense an edge in Parvathi's voice over his father's remarks. Ritu also glared at her husband. She didn't like her guest to be uncomfortable. Amit could not very much follow the undercurrents of tension arising all of a sudden. He got up to assist Lovely as she laid the table for lunch.

Chawla Bhai feeling cornered and realizing his folly remained silent. To ease tension and make her comfortable, he said, 'Parvathi beta we would like to meet your parents. I wish I knew you were coming. Ritu told me this morning and I thought it was a bit late to invite someone. Next time Ritu and I will ensure that we meet your parents as well.'

'Thanks Uncle. It happened so quickly. Auntie invited me day before yesterday and I accepted her offer. In any case my parents are invited for lunch today at *Mama's* place,' Parvathi explained.

'So you have quite a few relatives in Delhi. Your Mama is also in service?' Ritu asked.

'Yes he is the Joint Police Commissioner here, an IPS officer of Union Territories Cadre. One of my uncles is in the IAS working as Secretary to Government of India.'

Chawla sat upright and suddenly felt interested in her family. Addressing Ritu, he said, 'It's your fault. Next time we should meet Parvathi's parents and we all should have dinner together.' Turning towards Parvathi he said, 'Beta, we will drop in sometime and meet your parents.'

'It will be our pleasure Uncle. I do hope this meeting with my parents would be very soon.' Parvathi innocently said without realizing its connotation and looked at Anil who was making an effort to hide his smirk.

At this time Parvathi got a call from Nair on her mobile. Nair asked her the time she would like to be picked up since the car which had dropped her at Ritu Chawla's residence had gone back to Nair who was with a friend. Parvathi told her father that it might take another hour or so before she is finished with lunch. Nair offered to pick her on his way and it was decided that he would give a call on her mobile as he was about to reach Chawla's place so she could come out and join him.

Parvathi was seated next to Ritu and Chawla sat on her other side at the lunch table. Anil, Amit and Lovely sat opposite.

Chawla disconcerted by his last conversation with Omji thought of eliciting views of another young person Parvathi on career and home-life; considering it contextually relevant since Parvathi like Anil had studied abroad and now worked in a multi-national Company.

'Parvathi *beta*, you being the only child of your parents, how do you think they would cope up with your absence once you marry?'

'Well I think they are quite reconciled to the idea of being left alone after my marriage. They take it as a painful pre-destined future for them. As far as I know, they would be glad seeing me happy after marriage. Our family traditions do not suggest anything contrary to the widely accepted notions of marriage. The girl becomes an integral part of the family where she marries and looks after her new interests as well or perhaps more,' Parvathi answered. 'My Mom never for a minute thought of staying back in Kerala once my father got a permanent job in Delhi and has stayed here ever since, occasionally visiting her parents and other relatives. I do not think my parents have ideas different than what they have practiced. As for me, I have inherited their outlook,' she added.

'Are they happy allowing you to work?' Chawla asked.

'Yes of course. They treated me as an individual and in fact encouraged me to go for higher studies. They are delighted that I work for a good Company now.'

'And do you feel enthusiastic about assisting your Mom and Dad at home. I mean after a day's work of a different kind do you feel equally eager to help your mother at home?'

'Yes of course. I look forward to assist my mother in her household work. In fact in my family, my father also assists my mother after he comes back from office and on holidays he shares my mother's responsibilities. I love home after a day's hard work,' Parvathi replied.

Ritu looked at her husband Chawla Bhai accusingly without saying anything. Chawla knew he never moved a fly at home. Earlier it was Ritu and now Lovely doing all household work. Chawla realized he was treading on a mushy terrain and it was Anil who came to his rescue by changing the thread of the conversation.

'Parvathi, do you have any regrets coming back and joining this Company. You could have found yourself a decent job as you were studying in one of the top Universities of America?'

'No Anil, I don't have any regrets. In fact I am happy to come back to India. Perhaps I am not cut out for American way of life. I like my country, its culture and its way of life. I think I have a traditional mindset.' Parvathi wondered why Anil had asked this as he already knew her nature and inclination.

Soon she understood when Anil looked at his mother and approvingly said, 'That's commendable. Isn't it Mom?'

Ritu listening to the conversation and lost in thoughts about fashion show at Chandigarh nodded her head and said it was indeed commendable.

'Parvathi, it's really amazing how you can take interest in fashion industry possessing totally different qualifications and being engaged in a work of technical nature. How did you cultivate this interest?' Ritu wondered.

'Auntie, as a habit I try to keep myself abreast of developments in most of contemporary fields. My friend Rekha has provided me an eye for detail in the fashion field. Before I went to US my Mom wanted me to join Rekha's

Institute but I could not see a career for myself in this line. I am drawn towards computer industry in general. These days Textile and Fashion designing use computer software. I feel pleasure in being a part of Rekha's efforts, nothing more.' Parvathi honestly apprised her.

Lovely asked, 'Parvathi, after studying in America don't you miss here the fun you must have had there?'

Ritu was embarrassed again at such a puerile question but remained silent as Parvathi answered.

'I don't know what type of fun you are alluding to. As I understand fun, my life in US was no different than what I lead here now. I am a homely type, generally aware of my own responsibilities and expectations of others from me. My idea of fun is to enjoy in whatever I do.' Parvathi answered with a dismissive air.

Chawla was enjoying this conversation and feeling inquisitive asked, 'After high education abroad and developing an independent mind set how you feel about young boys and girls adapting to the conflicting demands imposed upon them by different generations within the family?'

Parvathi thought for a second as it was a tough one and answered, 'True, adapting to demands placed by different generations within the family does become an issue, though I feel it has more to do with individual character and personality. If one has affection for the family members and feels integrated with the family as one unit, then the edges emerging out of individual differences, though not completely erased are to a large extent softened. Even without higher studies or education abroad, these edges do spring up due to generational factors. But yes, the differences may accentuate after acquiring an independent bent of mind which higher studies and western way of life promotes. In nutshell I feel the response of a youngster would differ from person to person.'

Ritu, Chawla Bhai and Anil were impressed the way Parvathi explained. Anil beamed as Ritu and Chawla Bhai exchanged glance, appreciating Parvathi's intelligence. Amit and Lovely didn't feel the need to listen as they had missed the question.

Amit changed the topic and asked, 'Parvathi can you recall one incident in your university which you found hilarious.'

'Oh, there were so many. I recall one incident when during orientation a female student Alice asked the faculty member how much does it cost the boys to visit their hostels? The faculty member was taken aback and said the cost will depend on the purpose of the visit, ranging from expulsion to nothing. Then he asked Alice why she has asked this question. Alice narrated the incident saying in her previous college on the first day, the Dean addressing the students had pointed out some of the rules saying that the female dormitory would be out of bounds for all male-students, and the male dormitory to the female students. The Dean had said that anybody caught breaking this rule will be fined $20 for the first time, $60 for the second time and $ 200 for being caught the third time. At this point one male student had enquired how much would he be charged for a season pass? So Alice said that she was just wondering how much it would cost us here in this university.' Parvathi narrated the incident.

Everyone laughed after long. Anil asked, 'So what did the faculty member say?'

'Speechless for a moment, the faculty member clarified that University life is different from college life and there were no fines in that category but certainly students can be legally charged for their offences.' Everybody laughed again.

The sumptuous lunch lasting over two hours was coming to an end as Parvathi's mobile rang. She rose from her chair abruptly, thanked Chawla Bhai, Ritu and all the family members individually and sought Ritu's permission to go home. Chawla and Ritu enquired about the reason for rushing through, she mentioned about her father waiting at the gate.

'You can't do this Parvathi. Let me invite Mr Nair. We can have a cup of coffee together.' Chawla Bhai asked Anil to bring him in.

After initial hesitation, Nair accepted the invitation and was introduced to everyone in Chawla's family. He had met Anil earlier so he told Chawla about the nice Onam party which Anil and his colleagues hosted and how everyone missed Anil's family. Chawla looked at Anil's expressionless face. Nair appreciated Ritu for her interest in social work and fashion shows and told her that his daughter had been speaking very high about her.

Ritu was pleased no end. After half an hour, Nair and Parvathi left as Sunil Chawla and Ritu promised to visit them soon.

Anil led Nair and Parvathi to the gate and whispered in her ears 'You are through to the final.'

***

FIFTEEN

Ritu glanced at her watch, disengaged herself from the outstretched arms of her husband and rose from the bed.

'It's just six in the morning. Who can come home so early in the morning and press the call bell?' She thought. 'There has to be someone closely known to the family otherwise the guard would not have allowed use of the call bell.'

The bell rang again. The sound emanated from the middle of the door leading to their bedroom. Chawla stretched his arms, yawned and slumped back on the pillow. Ritu strutted out of the front door and asked the guard who informed her about the arrival of Chawla's younger brother Ramesh.

'Bhabhi, is Bhayya up?' Ramesh, breathless as if he had run a morning marathon, asked entering the sitting room.

'I'll wake him up. Is everything fine? You seem to be breathless.' Ritu apprehensively asked.

Chawla Bhai dressed in a gown sauntered in. Ramesh told Chawla and Ritu about the disappearance of his daughter Renu since last night. He informed them that Renu must have left sometime during the night and in the morning when he saw the door leading to her room open, he looked inside, there was no one on the bed and a letter was found kept on the dressing table. Ramesh handed over the letter to Chawla who started reading it as Ritu went into the kitchen to prepare tea.

The letter only mentioned that Renu didn't want to get engaged to Deepak Bhatia as she was in love with a boy named R.Madhvan from Jawaharlal Nehru University in Delhi and she was leaving with him for an unknown destination to get married and start her life afresh. She had further added that she would contact her family when she was satisfied that Madhvan would be accepted as a son-in-law and there was no need to panic or worry about her as she was safe with him.

Ritu entered the sitting room with the tray in her hand and Chawla passed on the letter to her.

'Who is this Madhvan?' Chawla asked.

'I have no clue what so ever. He must be her class mate in the university. I can find out more about him and his family from JNU,' Ramesh answered.

'Renu has mentioned something about her engagement to Deepak Bhatia. We have no information about Renu's engagement.' Ritu expressed surprise at her lack of knowledge about it.

'Bhabhi, nothing has been fixed. We like a Bhatia family in our neighborhood. They have good business of garments and their only son Deepak manages the shop with his father. They were sending feelers constantly for Renu's marriage with Deepak. I had asked Renu quite a few times and two days back I threatened her. She never mentioned she loved someone else.' Ramesh kept looking at the floor avoiding eye contact.

'Did anyone care to ask Renu about her choice?' Ritu asked.

'Her mother Poonam asked a few times. Renu only casually mentioned about her south Indian friend. Poonam did not take it seriously. And now she has eloped. Had I known she loved someone else I would never have agreed to her marriage with Deepak. Now what Bhatia family will think about us?' Ramesh started sobbing.

'Don't cry like a fool and just forget Bhatia. You agreed for her marriage with Deepak without asking Renu? Did your mind go away to chew grass in the field?' Chawla asked, irritated, in his own inimitable style.

'Yes *Bhayya*. Poonam and I committed this mistake. We never liked her friendship with the south Indian boy. She used to get phone calls from him. Lately, she had started coming late from JNU. That's why we did not take her into confidence while deciding her future.' Ramesh sheepishly explained.

It was decided that Chawla and Ramesh would go to JNU to track Madhvan and Renu.

Their visit yielded no information about their whereabouts except that R.Madhvan, a Tamil Brahmin from a suburb of Coimbatore used to stay in Sutlej Hostel in the campus till few months. He was a brilliant student and completed his studies in JNU last summer and no one knew where he worked now. Renu was his constant companion in JNU and their love affair, four years old, was known to all.

Having obtained Madhvan's home information from the University Office records Ramesh took the flight to Coimbatore, the nearest airport. His taxi traveled through narrow lanes teeming with people and cows. Dusty men pulled wooden carts loaded to the brim with sacks of stuff. Auto rickshaws zipped around like toy cars. Cyclists weaved in and out, tinkling their tiny bells. Ramesh remembered Paharganj and Chandni Chowk in Delhi and didn't see any difference.

The taxi driver stopped at an intersection and told Ramesh, 'from here you have to walk one hundred meters straight as car can not enter this narrow street.' He paid the driver and walked towards the narrow alley as a big fat cow stopped right in front of him.

'*Shoo*,' he told the animal, but it shook its head at him. He waved his brief case at her and the next thing he knew, he was flying in the air. He landed with a thud, crashing headlong into a parked motorcycle. The cow was on him snorting and digging its heels into the ground. The people around him in dhotis and shirts laughed at him. He got up slowly keeping an eye on the cow, dusting his pants, and made another attempt to walk ahead but the cow refused to let him pass.

It was only when a hawker selling bananas in a cart appeared that the cow turned around and made a beeline for him. Ramesh quickly took his steps and crossed into the narrowest part of the lane.

He stopped in front of a crumbling yellow building which bore the sign S. Ranganathan. Ramesh knocked on the door and the name plate almost fell off. He tried to tack it back as the door creaked open.

A white haired, dark complexioned man in his sixties, oily hair, wearing a lungi and shirt followed by his sick looking wife opened the door for him and Ramesh stepped in. The sitting room looked like it had been hit by a twister. The walls looked like they had not been painted in years and the room smelt like someone had been pissing in it. The old man introduced himself and his wife and asked the purpose of his visit.

On being told the entire story, the old man looked at his wife and said, 'Madhvan is a stubborn boy. He must have married his girl-friend by now. He didn't even care to inform us.'

'Do you have any idea about their whereabouts?' Ramesh asked.

'Madhvan is my son. I have his Singapore address where he teaches now. He was supposed to come home but perhaps due to some reasons he hasn't come here. I have no idea whether he is in India or has flown back to Singapore. I am a teacher in a local college here and do not have a telephone at my residence. I lost my mobile phone yesterday so Madhvan can not contact me till he comes home or calls me in College,' Madhvan's father thoughtfully said.

Ramesh was frustrated. He had expected to find Madhvan's whereabouts from his parents. He took the ignorance of his parents as an attempt to shield their son and was seething with anger.

'Do you have an idea where they are likely to go in India?' Ramesh asked, exasperated.

'I don't have any idea. Madhvan is a decent boy. He always stood first in class and has now found a very good job in National University of Singapore. He had taken fifteen days leave to come home. If he has married he must be visiting someplace I do not know,' Sunder Ranganathan nonchalantly answered.

'Decent? You stupid old man! You call him decent? He runs away with a girl, marries her and doesn't inform his parents or call them and still you call him decent? This is the kind of upbringing you gave him. Here you live in a slum and instigate your *decent* son to run away with a rich man's daughter so that you can bargain later. You are no help to me. I wish I should not have come here to this slum where you guys breed like mosquitoes and live like dogs. In our locality dogs sleep on Dunlop-pillow mattresses in mosquito free mansions.' Ramesh could not control himself and exploded.

'O Mister. Don't say a word against my son. I can not get a son like him. He is exceptionally brilliant and obedient. He has never gone against our wishes. If he has done something, then he must be having valid reasons to do so. I trust him completely. Ask your daughter who has eloped with a simple and naïve son of mine. That's what you have taught her. I don't bother about your money. You may leave my house now.' Sunder Ranganathan rose to show him the door.

Ramesh enquired from neighbors but could get nothing out except that Sunder and his son Madhvan were highly respected in their area. Sunder's father had been a freedom fighter and Sunder was the general secretary of District Freedom Fighters Association. Madhvan being their only child was raised with utmost care and love.

Ramesh called his wife and brother on phone and narrated the entire conversation with Madhvan's father and took the next flight back to Delhi.

****

'Now stop being an idiot. There is no point informing police. Renu is an adult. It would only invite bad publicity. You have messed up everything. All you can do now is to just wait for Renu to call,' Chawla told Ramesh, who had no option but to agree with his brother.

The blame game, round the corner, started with full intensity. Ramesh blamed his wife for her 'apathy' towards Renu, their daughter, and Poonam blamed her husband for rushing ahead with the marriage plan with the Bhatia family. Soon a common factor in the form of a poor South Indian family of Madhvan was discovered for berating. Motives started being attributed to Madhvan and his family of inadequate means.

'I know this boy Madhvan and his family planned the whole thing. They influenced our Renu's mind to take this step. All they want is money from us. How I wish Renu should have seen their designs and not taken this drastic step. Now she will regret all her life.' Poonam started sobbing.

'Now our child shall be a part of that slum I have seen with my own eyes. That will be her home. I feel sick remembering their smelly house,' Ramesh quipped.

'Forget the smelly house; I was always against sending her to JNU for higher education. You never listen to me. Our hopes are dashed to the ground. They must have married by now. Soon Renu will come back crying over spilt milk. This 'rogue' Madhvan and his family of cheats will present their demands and we will continue meeting those all our life. I know what they are up to.' Poonam moaned, shedding copious tears.

'If I find this boy I will twist his neck and kill him. He has destroyed our standing in the society. Soon our neighbors and relatives will get the scent of it. I am finished. I should have dragged that old couple to Delhi. This Madhvan would have begged me to release his parents,' Ramesh was boiling with rage.

In the evening the unexpected happened. Renu called her mother and told her that she was now married, happy and fine. They need not worry for her. She did not divulge further details and promised to call later.

Ramesh throwing the cautious words of his brother Chawla Bhai to winds went with a friend to see the Deputy Commissioner of Police, who advised him to install a caller identification device on phone and report to police about the telephone details when Renu calls. Ramesh did not lodge a formal report with the police.

The next call from Renu disclosed her location-Bangalore, where she was staying in a hotel after her wedding. After an informal enquiry, police relying on their statements, refused to intervene as Renu and Madhvan were adults and had married intentionally without any duress or influence.

The marriage court had already put its seal of approval and they were legally husband and wife.

Not able to cut any ice with the police and pained at developments, Ramesh lost his sense of propriety. The pain emptied his mind of everything else, and feelings of love, hate, envy and jealousy were bleached from his mind and was left with an excruciating agony filling each pore of his body. The wailing of his wife added to his pain further and guided by wrong advice embarked upon a path with inherent dangers. He contacted the criminal gang in the area, one run by Munna Pehalwan, pleaded to undo the 'injustice' done by Madhvan and his family to him and paid fifty thousand rupees as advance.

Madhvan's father Sunder was the first to receive a threat followed by a visit from two goons who physically thrashed him and ransacked his house.

Beating up of Madhvan's father and damage to his house caused a great stir in the suburbs and in Coimbatore. Sunder was a widely respected man from a family of freedom fighters and immediate checking at railway stations, airport and highways led to the arrest of one of the two criminals fleeing the city. It was a matter of time before the criminal started singing and named Munna Pehalwan's criminal gang in Delhi behind the attack. The media in South reported the incident.

Another set of criminals reached Bangalore but minutes before they could lay their hands on Madhvan and Renu, the criminals got to know about the arrest of one of their men in Coimbatore, sensed trouble and disappeared.

The Home Minister of Tamilnadu followed the developments closely and spoke to the Home Minister in Delhi. As the matter took a political shape, Delhi Police Commissioner was summoned in the Home Ministry who in turn deputed the Joint Police Commissioner O.P

Menon to solve the riddle and nab the culprits. Few hours later Munna Pehalwan was behind bars and the Joint Police Commissioner, Delhi, Mr. Menon was sitting with Ramesh Chawla and his wife Poonam.

Arrest of Ramesh sent tremors into the Chawla household, the business area and in political circles. As Ramesh was charged under Sec-307 Indian Penal Code for attempt to murder Sunder, it shook his entire family and the media expectedly gave a North-South angle to the whole story.

The press flashed the news on the first page and TV news channels 'breaking news' announced the attack on an old freedom fighter funded by a business man of Karol Bagh in Delhi to avenge his daughter's love affair and marriage with a south Indian boy Madhvan. Few channels even announced Sunder was dead.

The TV men aimed their cameras at Ramesh Chawla's home, tried to interview his wife Poonam who refused to come out. The All India Tamil Forum, a loose knit and less known apex organization of Tamilians in Delhi, seized the opportunity to highlight their presence by organizing boys to stand at the gate of Ramesh Chawla's house with posters denouncing the attack and flashing 'Down with north Indian Racism.'

Ritu, stunned at the developments, cursed her fate and the stupidity of her husband's brother and refused to be drawn into any controversy. When asked by friends, she shook her hands off and claimed that her husband Sunil Chawla and his brother Ramesh Chawla had nothing in common as both had separate business interests and lived lives of their own. Chawla thought of going to his brother's house but his bottled up anger did not allow him to do so. 'After all Ramesh did not listen to me, planned a murderous attack on another family and destroyed the family name. Let him pay for his sins.' Chawla Bhai thought. He asked Om*ji* instead to see that Ramesh gets bail.

Parvathi got to know about the developments through newspapers next day. The papers carried details about the family of Ramesh Chawla which included the name of Sunil Chawla known as Chawla Bhai. Anil was highly embarrassed and felt concerned about his own alliance with a south Indian family. He met Parvathi and convinced her that his family had nothing to do with this incident and it was his uncle's crazy and stupid act, uncharacteristic of the family culture and traditions. Mr Menon, the Joint Police Commissioner casually mentioned the story to his sister Lathika and brother in law Nair few hours after the arrest of Ramesh. Lathika and Nair grew further apprehensive about the Punjabi families of Delhi and their past history. Parvathi sensing her parent's apprehensions about North Indian families tried her best to take the edge off their indignation and succeeded considerably. She informed them that it was an individual act and Chawla family or their community had nothing to do with it.

Madhvan and Renu, throwing their fears aside rushed to Coimbatore and stayed with Sunder in the hospital. Madhvan, a gentleman, handled the issue with rare poise and equanimity. He refused to comment either on his marriage, which he called his personal affair or on the dastardly attack on his father, which he did not connect to any North-South divide but called it an act of a desperate father. It helped the controversy die down.

Ramesh could not get bail from the court and was put in judicial custody for seven days which meant he had to stay as an under-trial in Tihar Jail.

After staying for three days with Sunder in the hospital at Coimbatore, Renu and Madhvan reached Delhi. Renu took Madhvan with her to her house and introduced him to her distraught mother and few relatives present. Madhvan touched her feet and sought her blessings. Sobbing hysterically, Poonam blessed him. Later, Madhvan and Renu requested Omji to arrange for their visit to Tihar Jail to see Ramesh.

When Madhvan and Renu accompanied by Omji entered the visitor's area they saw Ramesh walk down the corridor, head bent down and fresh grey stubble on face, Renu started crying as Madhvan held her. Om*ji* introduced Madhvan to Ramesh and walked away to a distance.

Renu and Madhvan sought his blessings and blamed themselves for his present state. Ramesh looked up, saw his daughter in a red saree with red *sindoor* in her hair, could not control his emotions and broke down. He stretched his hand to bless Renu and Madhvan; but his face said more though his hands failed to touch their head. Madhvan and Renu begged to be forgiven as Ramesh enquired about his father in Coimbatore. He admitted he never wanted any physical harm should come to Sunder and out of anguish he had arranged for a threat to be delivered but the criminals crossed their mandate. He owned full responsibility for whatever happened there and begged to forgive him. No one could say anything as all three cried till the visiting hours were over.

Few days later Ramesh was granted bail by the High Court.

The biggest casualty was the social standing of Ritu and Sunil Chawla and they felt that their world was no longer the same. Jolted by the events in the family, Chawla and Ritu decided that before it's too late, they should look for a suitable girl for Anil and make him tie the knot. Such events do not augur well for finding a decent match for Anil, Chawla thought.

***

SIXTEEN

Om*ji* was not coming to Gymkhana for the last one week. It was difficult to say who was surprised more; Chawla Bhai or other members of the club. After all, Om*ji* was Chawla's conscience keeper and trouble shooter but more important, provided him company every evening after a tiring and monotonous day at the saree showrooms. Om*ji* had missed his evening visit to Gymkhana six times in his last twenty years. Twice, when his son and daughter got married and rest four when he was down with illness. His presence was as much a part of the Club as were its painted-walls, chairs, waiters or the bartender. These days he was more conspicuous by his absence.

It was only when several SMS and missed calls during last twelve hours could not bring out any response; Chawla Bhai turned his car towards Civil Lines in Delhi where Om*ji* lived. He reached the gate, promptly opened by the security man outside and Chawla's car drove through the long driveway up to the porch. Omji himself walked up to the door to receive him as the guard had informed him on intercom about Chawla's arrival.

Looking at Om*ji* any one would have guessed that there was something awfully bad. Om*ji* in unkempt grey hair looked as he had not bathed and shaved for last two days.

Om*ji* hugged his friend without uttering a single word as if he had taken a vow not to speak to anyone and escorted him to the sitting room.

'Oye, what is the problem? What are you up to?' Chawla asked.

'Chawla Bhai, it seems God has snatched my happiness by giving me this pain that would last my whole life.'

'Tell me what I can do Om*ji*. What has happened?'

'I won't be able to rest in peace now. Her presence will constantly remind me of her pain.'

'*Arrey*, what happened? Can't you tell straight? Why do you talk in riddles?' Chawla visibly irritated asked.

'Didn't I tell you about my daughter Dolly in the club? She was about to be divorced last year because of undue interference from my wife but somehow things could be managed. Now she has come back from her husband. She says she would not go back. My son in-law says he doesn't want a wife who looks towards her mother all the time and hardly cares about him and his family. Last year I had mediated and solved a crisis. But it seems impossible now.'

'What is the stand taken by the parents of your son-in-law? Can't they help solve the problem?' Chawla asked.

'Chawla Bhai I didn't tell you, I spent more than a crore to get my daughter married in this Punjabi Luthra family thinking they are nice people. I always blamed my wife for interfering in the life of my daughter and son-in-law. I agree, she did interfere unduly, but my daughter was also being harassed and beaten up by her husband and in laws. Our daughter Dolly told us they even tried to burn her alive while she was sleeping by leaving the gas cylinder on as they went out. Only God saved her as their neighbor dropped by to make a phone call, smelled the gas leakage, brought her out of the house and opened all doors and windows. The Luthra family is demanding another fifty lakhs and a flat in South Delhi. I don't have that kind of money Chawla Bhai. What should I do? Should I go to the police?'

'Relax, you can lodge a report with police and drag them to the court but that's not going to ensure your daughter's future with her husband. First, you have to decide whether you want to come to a settlement with them or take revenge.' Chawla tried to reason with him.

'See, under no circumstances my daughter is going back there. They will kill her. Had it just been the money, I would have sold this house and pawned myself to ensure my child's happiness. But it's her life I fear most,' Omji said with tears in his eyes.

'We will teach this 'mother-fucker' and his son a lesson Omji. They are a blot on our community. You relax. Let me think over it. But be sure, there would be no settlement with them after that,' Chawla said.

'No question of a settlement with them. I wish Luthra had married his son into Angad Singh's family and tried to act this way. He would have torn them to pieces,' Omji said in anger.

'Who is Angad Singh?'

'The mafia-politician from Patna. One who sent his proposal for your son Anil.'

Suddenly Chawla remembered Angad Singh's son and the armed men outside his showroom and he felt a scary sensation run through his body as his hair stood raised.

'Don't worry Om*ji*. This time it's my turn to help you. I'll think something. But let's go to the club and have a drink.'

Om*ji* took half an hour to shave and shower. In exactly forty five minutes they were driving towards the club as Chawla Bhai's mind raced to find a solution and he found it before reaching the club.

Chawla called Ritu and obtained Parvathi's mobile number. Then he called Parvathi and asked for her father Mr Nair's whereabouts and his mobile number.

After fortifying himself with whiskey Chawla called Nair who was still in office.

'Nair Sahib, do you remember me? I am Anil's father Sunil Chawla. We met when you came to pick Parvathi from my place.'

'Yes of course Chawla*ji*. I am not that old to forget you and your beautiful wife. It's a pleasure talking to you. I was telling Parvathi the other day we should have you at our home. *Kaise yaad kiya*?'

'Why do you have to work so hard? In case are not awfully busy give us company here. We are not far from Central Secretariat. I am sending my driver with the car. You can follow him. We'll have drink and dinner here. I want to discuss something with you. If you want we can come over to you.'

'Chawla Bhai, it's so kind of you. I was about to leave for home. Give me half an hour to finish my pending work. Don't send your driver; I'll come on my own.' Nair wondered what could be the subject of discussion all of a sudden.

As Nair settled in the cozy corner reserved for Omji and Chawla, downed a couple of pegs, Chawla said, '*Nair Sahib*, I just met you once and you would think I am bringing my problem to you. But the matter is serious and urgent. Parvathi told us that your brother-in-law is a senior officer in Delhi Police. We need his help.'

Chawla narrated the entire sequence of events about Omji's daughter and her in laws.

'I thought such problems arise only between two different communities but it is surprising how Punjabis are quarrelling amongst themselves,' Nair sarcastically said.

“Nair *Sahib*, communities have nothing to do with such problems, it is human nature which is responsible for all this. Our greed overtakes us and we act like demons.' Chawla tried to explain.

'And we all prefer Punjabi or Malayali families for our children thinking that it would guarantee and ensure their happiness. How short sighted we are,' Nair sighed.

'True. But Nair *Sahib* how can we help Om*ji* now? His daughter doesn't want to go back to her husband fearing threat to her life.

'Do you want to criminally proceed against them, I mean against your son in law and his family?' Nair asked, and advised, 'If you think so, then go to my brother in law who can advise best. He is the Joint Commissioner of Police here.'

'Let us meet him tomorrow morning. Is it fine Om*ji*?' Chawla asked.

Nair called Menon, the Joint Commissioner of Police and fixed next morning's appointment at ten.

Om*ji* and Chawla reached the Police Headquarters. Menon patiently listened to the entire incident and advised Omji to lodge a report with the police without delay and leave the rest to Police. When everyone was about to leave Menon said, 'Marriage is a tricky issue, especially in arranged types. One should go beyond caste, community, region or religion and should find out the antecedents of the family before taking the plunge. Everyday police receives scores of complaints regarding matrimonial harassment, including deaths.'

Om*ji* and his daughter filed a formal report with the Police at the local Police Station. They narrated the entire sequence of incidents in their report alleging extortion, threats, cruelty, dowry and attempt to murder. The message to the Police station from Menon took care of the rest. The police charged Luthra family including Om*ji*'s son-in -law under sections 498A for mental and physical torture, Sec-323 for causing hurt, Sec-341 for willful restraint, Sec-354 for outraging modesty, Sec-506 for criminal intimidation and Sec-307 for attempt to murder and arrested the father and son from their residence. Their bail application was refused and they were remanded for fourteen days to police custody.

The arrests created quite a ruckus in the social and business circles of both families. A number of people from their own community offered to mediate but Omji considered it too late and politely declined their offer. The media was fast to catch up the story and interviewed Dolly who narrated the ghastly details of her married life. With added spice, the TV channels showed atrocities on Dolly and the Women's organizations and social activists soon took up her cause and the family matter got blown up into larger issues of dowry, bride burning, wife beating and harassment of women.

As expected, the incident provided bad publicity to the main actors and their families in the drama and unjustifiably placed the entire community under the scanner. No involvement of a different community in this drama turned out to be a silver lining. For Chawla, this was a second incident within a short span of time. Earlier it was his brother who gave him sleepless nights and now the family matter of his closest friend provided him discomfort. His social standing in the club plummeted fast.

Ritu could see her social invitations and kitty parties thinning out. The business community of Old Delhi had unnecessarily come under media glare. The Punjabi community of the area rightfully tried to shake off the media by diverting media attention to the two families rather than the whole community. It resulted in more focused attention on few families in the area and Chawla Bhai's family happened to be one of them, though indirectly. In clubs and parties, women envious of Ritu found ammunition to attack her and her highflying life style, gradually implicating her children and questioning their upbringing and sub culture.

'This is bound to happen in families where the lady of the house keeps flitting from one party to another and men are busy counting money.' Ritu heard a club member from Karolbagh, say.

'They may send their son or daughter abroad but it won't change the family's culture or thinking'. Another friend of her commented.

'A false and frivolous life style leads to such incidents when daughters elope and son in law tortures his wife physically and mentally.' Ritu heard a lady from Model town say, and felt distressed.

Ritu felt sad at the turn of events and it took away the swagger from her gait and pride from her demeanor. She mostly stayed at home and spent time either watching television or reading magazines.

Parvathi sensed something was wrong as Ritu had stopped calling on her mobile. It seemed Ritu had lost interest in the fashion show at Chandigarh. She called Ritu who requested her to come over. Ritu told her all about her feelings and shared her misery with Parvathi.

'But Aunty, this is absolutely unjustified and wrong. How your families or an entire community can be blamed for whatever has happened?' Parvathi asked.

'But this is what's happening. I don't feel like going anywhere these days.' Ritu answered. 'Everyone looks at me as if I am one of the culprits,' she added.

'Aunty, can I accompany you to your clubs and parties for few days. Let me handle this. I would suggest don't stop going there as it would further lead to bitching and gossip behind your back. Those jealous of you are trying to hit you below the belt.'

Two days later, Ritu accompanied with Parvathi attended the book release and felicitation event at India International Centre, where many of Ritu's friends and club members were present. The media was present in full number.

The book '*Changing Women Culture in India*' was written by a close friend of Ritu and during the interactive session a lady asked, 'How do you see the transition of Indian women from kitchen and home to office and their social circle affect the upbringing of children?'

Ritu's old class-mate asked, 'We have seen how parents go for arranged marriages within their communities trying to ensure their daughter's happiness and stability but they are tortured for money. Is the concept of arranged marriage dead?'

Another question was asked by a media person, 'we recently saw daughters run away with their lovers to avoid marriages being fixed for perpetuation of caste and community bonds. Is the sanctity of marriage as an institution dying?'

'By socializing and showing off, aren't the new rich women trying to cover up their complex and affecting their family culture by not being with children at home when they need them most?' A correspondent from *Free Press Today* asked, prompted by Ritu's competitor Neha who lost to her in one of the competitions at the club.

Ritu flinched as she thought the question was an insidious attack on her family and her community in general. Parvathi raised her hand and asked for the floating portable mike to address the gathering.

'We have this beautiful habit of generalizing things when we do not wish to strain our brain cells any more. If a press reporter is charged of mental and physical harassment of his wife does it mean every press person is guilty? If a person from a Haryana village kills his daughter because she went against the family to marry someone she loved, does it make every person from Haryana a murderer? We like to do media trial before the actual trial begins in court. Isolated acts are generalized and we climb up the moral pillar at once and start pronouncing judgments blaming the whole community, caste or region. A look at the matrimonial advertisements in the newspapers would show our own preference for narrow considerations of caste, color, creed and region. The advertisements for brides and grooms and marriages happening all around do show that people have faith in the institution of marriage and not an erosion of the faith. Why do we have to take a narrow view of everything? I'm a Keralite, and I and one Punjabi boy whose mother is sitting beside me work for the same Company. I met this lady Mrs. Ritu Chawla at a fashion show few months back. We have grown fond of each other now and share a good relationship based on mutual respect. Rituji is a great lady who never for a moment hesitated in taking me into her fold despite me being a non-Punjabi and a non-Delhite. My parents are not in business and we don't have too much money either. But she or her husband never let me feel as an outsider in their family and she likes and supports me from heart. She finds time to attend our functions and invites me home for lunch and dinner. Why these incidents are not reported? I would like the media here also to report how such friendships are evolved and not just generalize about the institution of marriage on the basis of few isolated incidents here and there. I am strongly against what happened in the two cases involving a particular community of Old Delhi. Very few are now interested to know that the girl who eloped recently married her boy friend of four years; a south Indian, decently employed in Singapore and happily settled. The boy or his family did not raise any demand for money and they are living happily now. No doubt it was a wrong act on the part of a desperate father to try and browbeat the boy's family and he would face trial in court. But let the law take its own course and don't pronounce a judgment before the court does it. And the mother of the girl who eloped and married is a housewife who hardly steps out of her home, not a working lady who has spoiled her daughter's mindset or upbringing.'

There were claps as Parvathi lashed at the detractors.

She continued. 'Women going out of their kitchen and home to work and socialize can never adversely impact their children's upbringing. Had it been so, all these ladies sitting here and the young girls working for the media and present here will either provide abnormal upbringing to their children or be one, themselves. What is wrong if today a woman wishes to express herself through dress, words and her acts in the society? Why do we want a social 'Talibisation' in this free country? Who has prescribed this role for women that she has to confine herself to home? Mrs. Ritu Chawla raised her children beautifully and now when she is relatively free from her domestic responsibilities she moves in society, expresses her the way she likes and encourages young people like me. Why should anyone be jealous at what she is doing and pass snide remarks? Are those who are sitting here sure they have raised their children as well as Mrs. Ritu Chawla? I studied in America and came home just because I love the society and culture here. There are so many like me who return and contribute towards their culture and society. We all must be proud of ourselves that we are doing something worthwhile and for a cause. The author who has written this book deserve all praise for her convictions rather than suffer pangs of jealousy from those who could not write and don't wish others to do a creative work. Lastly, I would request with all humility that do not denigrate yourself, others and your entire community by pointing fingers just because someone did something wrong in Punjab or Pondicherry. I am sorry I took lot of your time and became emotional as I could not see my Ritu Aunty depressed just because of few preposterous assumptions made by diseased minds.'

There were clapping all around and Ritu, with her eyes wet, hugged her and kissed Parvathi's cheek as the clapping continued. Ritu saw few women sneak out from the hall. Parvathi's exposition remained the high point of the evening and at Tea, she and Ritu were mobbed and appreciated again and again.

The confidence and conceit returned in Ritu's gait as Parvathi rejoiced to see her happy.

The Press present at the occasion, carried Parvathi's bare knuckled verbal assault and lashing in the newspapers. She became an instant hit with the women as Ritu regained her poise and respect. Ritu dropped Parvathi outside her home and left thinking about Parvathi's exposition. She told Chawla Bhai everything at night and he was happy after long.

Parvathi did not call Anil as she wanted that he should come to know through other sources which he did next morning, congratulated her and asked her to join him at the discotheque at ten in the night to have a blast and celebrate her instant celebrity status with his mother's friends.

Their stay at the discotheque couldn't be for long and resulted in a minor quarrel between them. While Anil and Parvathi were dancing on the floor a female colleague from Global Logix dancing in drunken stupor, grabbed Anil's arm, whispered in his ear and kissed him on the cheek. Anil was dumbfounded.

She was one of the girls who had a very short time pass relationship with him before Anil got to know Parvathi.

Parvathi watched it in horror and couldn't control herself, left the dance floor and sat in one corner. Anil joined her and tried to calm her down explaining that she worked in the office but she had never been more than a casual acquaintance.

'So any girl can grab your arm, pull you toward her and plant a kiss on your cheek? You want me to accept this crap?' Parvathi exploded.

'Of course not dear, but what's my fault? Have you ever seen her anywhere near me? She is drunk.' Anil tried to put his arm around Parvathi but she shook it away.

'What did she say in your ear?'

'She congratulated me and jokingly said she had missed her chance. I couldn't have heard because of the loud music that's why she came close and said it in my ear.' Anil explained.

It made sense to Parvathi and helped her calm down. She had heard about several girls liking Anil before he came into contact with her. She didn't mind that. But she had made it clear to Anil that he could either have Parvathi as his friend or any of the girls from the Company. Anil assured her about the first option.

She reminded Anil about his promise and allowed him to put his hands on her shoulder.

Anil looked at the two big advertisement sign boards on the road, smiled and thought, 'man before marriage is like Airtel.... '*Aisi Azaadi Aur Kahan*'. After marriage he is like Vodafone.... 'Wherever you go our network follows.'

***

SEVENTEEN

It promised to be a pleasant and peaceful night. Ritu and Chawla Bhai after months stayed at home just by themselves. Amit and Lovely had gone out of Delhi and Anil left on a short trip to Mumbai. The day had gone well. After several days of family tension, both Ritu and Sunil Chawla felt peace within.

Chawla made a glass of whiskey for himself, poured Bordeaux for Ritu and they sat on the terrace in the moonlight.

'After ages we are together like this Ritu. House looks so lonely without children.' Chawla mused.

'Yes dear, it's something or the other which keeps us busy. You remember when we had moon-lit dinner last?'

'No I don't.'

'It was during our last visit to Kovalam Beach. That was three years back. Anil was in US and Amit and Lovely had stayed back for business. You, I and Om*ji*'s family were in Kovalam and just the two of us sat in the hotel balcony at night.' Ritu reminded him.

'Yes, now I remember. Om*ji* and his family had gone to visit Kanyakumari and stayed back at their friends place.'

Chawla suddenly remembered their quarrel in the hotel balcony that night. He was alone with Ritu in the balcony when Ritu had mentioned about the guests staying in the adjoining room and how the man kissed his wife or whosoever she was every time he went out. Ritu had complained that Chawla Bhai should take a lesson or two from this man and kiss the way he does. All he had said was he didn't know the woman next door so how could he possibly do that. It had resulted in few broken pieces of hotel cutlery and later he had to pacify her for long, singing Hindi movie love songs in the moon light.

'How time flies Sunil. Children are settled. These last three years have been quite eventful,' Ritu thoughtfully said.

'Now as you mentioned Kovalam it reminded me of Parvathi. What do you think about her?' Chawla cautiously broached the subject.

Chawla suspected his son Anil liked Parvathi. His experienced eyes had noted sudden flashes of spark in his son's eyes when Parvathi had come for Lunch. Someone had earlier reported that Anil was seen with a south Indian beautiful girl and Lovely had in fact confronted Anil and he denied. He remembered Rekha's fashion show where Anil showed up. Chawla never spoke about it because he wasn't sure. In fact, Chawla had started liking Parvathi after meeting and talking to her.

'Oh definitely she is a very good girl. I have met her so many times and I found her very down to earth, courteous and intelligent. Doesn't she look like Vidya Balan?' Ritu asked.

'Who is Vidya Balan? Do I know her?' Chawla scratched his head.

'Oh my little stupid husband, you don't know her? She is an actress. Ok, Leave it.' Ritu laughed and continued, 'What made you think about Parvathi at this time?'

'Nothing, all of a sudden it crossed my mind how Anil and Parvathi would look together. What do you think about her? She has studied in USA like Anil. Works in the same Company and she looks very grounded to me. She answered all my questions during lunch with utmost sincerity and thought. How she lashed at the critics during the book launch party? I have kept the press clippings about her verbal assault.' Chawla looked at Ritu's face trying to read her expressions.

'To be honest Sunil, the idea did cross my mind few times. I do get positive vibes from her. I feel that we must explore this possibility. But only if Anil agrees to it otherwise it will lead to complications in his official life,' Parvathi thoughtfully said and added, 'Parvathi is the kind of girl I always wanted for Anil and for our family. She is the right mix of tradition and modernity, very intelligent and respectful.'

'So, who would talk to Anil, you or I?'

'I can talk to him on his return.' Ritu looked keen and eager to talk to Anil.

'But suppose Parvathi or her parents don't agree or we don't find them suitable for our family in some way?' Chawla asked.

'Then we shall look elsewhere. But let us have Anil's views on the subject. I feel lucky today.' Ritu smiled.

'Then you call Anil right now and ask him. Aren't you feeling lucky?' Chawla started dialing Anil's mobile from the land line. The moment he heard Anil answer he handed the phone to Ritu.

'*Beta*, how was your journey? We were just sitting alone on the terrace in the moon light. Amit and Lovely have gone out. Just remembered you and the great family lunch we had with Parvathi last Sunday.' Ritu cautiously proceeded.

'Yes Mom, flight landed on time. Its good Papa is at home. Enjoy yourself; you hardly get time to sit with each other..... I shall be back by evening flight tomorrow,' Anil replied. He agreed, 'yeah, it was a great family lunch.'

'If you don't mind can I ask you one thing Beta?' Ritu said.

'Yes Mom'

'What do you think about Parvathi?' Ritu asked.

'What do you mean Mom? I couldn't follow.' Anil expected this question but not at this time.

'In fact we were just talking about how you and Parvathi look together. We feel she might be the right choice for you and our family,' Ritu said. She waited for any reaction and finding none added, 'But of course if you agree with our assessment about her and like Parvathi in every sense.'

Anil discovered his heart was pounding with excitement and his breathing had become difficult. His mind was numb due to the suddenness of the offer. He paused for a moment, tried to gather his wits and spoke.

'Well, I leave it to you Mom. If both of you are happy with Parvathi, I am fine with it. You can go ahead. I have met her and I find her good natured and likeminded. I liked the way she spoke on your behalf and became an instant hit. She is very intelligent, that's all I can say.' Anil mustered words making considerable effort to sound normal.

Ritu handed back the phone to Chawla, 'Beta, I like the way she thinks and she appears very down to earth. She is intelligent and the kind of girl you would perhaps approve and be happy with. In case you agree to our proposal we would find out more about her parents and family and pursue the matter further.'

'But Papa they are Keralites. I personally have no problem with this. All I would suggest is that later these issues about which we know right in the beginning should not become important factors prejudicing decisions.' Anil stated to make sure nothing goes wrong later because of the south Indian factor, and continued, 'I have already told Mom to go ahead.'

'Great. They have been living in Delhi for last thirty years or so. I do not consider their origin a very important factor. Do I become a Pakistani as I migrated in 1947 to what is now India? I am as Indian as you or Parvathi is.'

Anil laughed loudly at the analogy and said, 'No Papa you are not a Pakistani but very much an Indian as West Punjab was a part of India before independence. So go ahead, you and Mom can pursue the matter further with her parents the way you like.'

'Ok *beta*. See you tomorrow.'

'See you Papa.'

Immediately Anil dialed Parvathi's mobile and broke the news to her who sounded equally excited about the progress. They decided to meet soon after his return. He suggested Maurya Hotel at seven pm immediately after his flight would land at IGI airport which was instantly agreed.

Parvathi, dressed in a shining dark blue saree with mirror work, waited for him in the Lobby of Maurya Hotel on Sardar Patel Marg. She had put flower in her hair. Being really excited she couldn't wait to hear from Anil about his conversation with his parents. Though Anil had immediately told her about his parent's feelings for her, yet she wanted to hear every word from him, face to face.

Anil's flight landed on time and reached hotel quite early as the traffic was thin. Dressed in a casual navy blue shirt and jeans, he hugged Parvathi and asked her to wait in the lobby as he wanted to use the washroom. Parvathi saw her maternal uncle enter the hotel with a friend. There was no way she could avoid being seen. Her 'mama' being a police officer surveyed the lobby with a quick roll of his eye and sighting his niece stepped forward, hugged her and introduced her to his friend. Parvathi told him about her wait for her colleague from office for a business talk. Before her uncle could leave her for some restaurant, Anil returned and said, 'come on love, lets go to Dum Pukht restaurant. I had booked a table for us.'

Her uncle heard him say 'love' and smiled. Parvathi was nervous and speechless. Having no option, she introduced Anil as her friend and colleague from the office and her maternal uncle as Mr Menon from the police department.

Mr Menon smiled and while leaving said, 'ok love, enjoy your dinner.'

Parvathi was quite shaken and told Anil that her uncle being a police officer would put two and two together and understand their closeness. Anil didn't care much about it and guided her to a vacant table in the right corner where they sat close to each other. Why should Anil care when his parents liked Parvathi.

"So, what's up?' Parvathi asked smiling.

'I told you everything. My parents have taken my consent. Soon our parents are going to meet. I don't know when and where the meeting will take place. But it's very important we prepare them for the meeting.' Anil thoughtfully answered taking Parvathi's hand in his.

'How do we prepare them? Do you mean I should tell my parents about us now?' Parvathi enquired.

'Not exactly, I mean when my parents contact your parents and meet, there shouldn't be any misunderstanding. It's always better to brief them beforehand.' Anil reflected.

'How do I brief my parents? I have to tell them about my inclination,' Parvathi said looking at Anil's face.

'Ok, go ahead, tell them. You are the best judge. Your father has met my parents once in different circumstances. Marriage alliance is special. But once you tell them about your wish, do brief them about my parents properly so that nothing untoward happens during their meeting. See, my father runs a traditional business and Mom as you know likes partying and socializing. You must have realized by now they are good and straight people. Their outlook towards life is different from others,' Anil explained, and added, 'So is the case with your parents. They are simple, straightforward and are deep rooted in their culture. All we want is differences of culture, education and financial status should not come in the way.'

'True. I'll try to make my parents deal with the entire issue objectively.'

'Precisely, that's what I want.' Anil felt relieved.

Anil told her about his work in Mumbai, Parvathi apprised him about her meeting with Rekha. She told Anil about possibility of Rekha inviting Ritu once again for the Chandigarh Fashion event, though not as the Chief Guest. Anil did not comment as he became engrossed enjoying his favorite 'ghazal' being sung by the hotel singer.

****

Joint Police Commissioner Menon was sure Anil was more than a colleague for his niece, Parvathi. 'Since when, professionals have started meeting their lady colleague all alone in restaurants at night, and addressing her as 'Love'? Maybe times have changed and I have grown old,' Menon thought. He called the waiter in Bukhara restaurant and asked him to locate a lady in a shining blue saree and a man with her dressed in blue shirt and jeans. Menon's police training and experience had equipped him with an uncanny ability to remember the attire of a person he met. How could he forget his niece and the man with her?

Within next ten minutes he got to know that his niece was having dinner in 'Dumpukht', another restaurant in the same hotel. Being a senior police officer and a regular customer, he knew the Duty Manager and asked him to keep an eye on the man sitting with the lady in 'Dumpukht' restaurant. He told him that the man is one of the suspects police is looking for and as a police officer he needs to know what he is doing and the time when he leaves. Menon believed in sharing information on need to know basis.

The Assistant Manager on duty was too glad to report back everything including their separate seating through his men at the restaurant and when Anil enjoyed the 'ghazal' singing, Menon was being informed. Nothing came to Menon's knowledge which could raise his suspicions further.

Menon told his sister and brother in law Nair the next day. Lathika and Nair told Menon that Anil is a colleague of Parvathi and a good man coming from a decent family. Lathika and Nair told him about their meeting with Anil and his entire family when he had picked up Parvathi from their home. Menon trusted his brother in law and sister's judgment.

***

EIGHTEEN

As Nair entered the gate of his ground floor flat, he found Mrs. Bhasin's dog, 'baccha' strapped. It was a good sign. The dog looked with a friendly squint, yawned and slumped on his side to catch up with his sleep. Nair knew it was going to be a good day for him.

Like every morning Nair and Lathika sat at their computer table looking for grooms on Keralamatrimony.com. Parvathi brought tea for them but today she sat beside her mother. Lathika and Nair were a bit surprised and stopped their search. Parvathi keen to start a conversation on their search for a groom, asked, 'Mom, what do you look at every morning on this matrimonial web site?'

Before Lathika could answer Nair said, 'Like all parents we are looking for a suitable boy for you.'

"But why only Keralamatrimony dot com, I have never seen you searching elsewhere,' said Parvathi with a smile.

'It's because we would like a Kerala boy for our dear daughter,' Nair replied affectionately.

'Suppose instead of a Kerala guy I like a north Indian?' Parvathi asked.

'It's fine with us if he and his family are good. But I don't think we can find one in Delhi. If the boy is good, the family may be rotten or vice versa. At least I haven't seen anywhere here where the boy and the family are both good. More importantly why should a north Indian family seek a south Indian daughter-in-law? Do you have anyone in mind?' Lathika was curious.

'Yes I do, but what do you think about the guys you met at Onam party? They were from my Company.' Parvathi cautiously broached the subject without naming anyone in particular.

'They were all nice. I don't remember anyone except Anil who came home for dinner the other day. I have met his parents when I picked you from their home. Anil is good, though we don't know much about his family except that they are from Delhi and have a business of their own. Knowing someone is different than looking for a suitable family for your own daughter,' Nair said.

'I have a feeling he likes me and my family,' Parvathi blushed and coyly said.

Lathika excited by the prospects asked, 'Did he say something? How do you know?'

'I have a feeling the way he has been praising both of you and liked the dinner Mom cooked. He mentioned to one of our common friends that he liked me,' Parvathi lied, and added, 'I have met his mother during Rekha's fashion show and she once invited me to their home for lunch. I met her again during a book launch party. She likes me a lot.'

'And do you like Anil,' Nair removing his spectacles asked what he considered most important.

'Well, I find him a decent person and easy to talk to. He has a pleasing personality and we share common interests. I feel comfortable with him.' Parvathi looked down feeling shy admitting the fact to her parents.

'Is he the same guy who was having dinner with you at Maurya?' Lathika asked Parvathi as Nair smiled. Lathika remembered her brother's observations in Maurya hotel.

'Yes,' Parvathi coyly admitted the fact.

'And what about his parents, do they like you?' Nair asked.

'I found them understanding. Don't know for sure.'

Lathika and Nair looked at each other and smiled, understanding their daughter's choice. They felt that their daughter was in love with Anil. Lathika had liked Anil after he dined at their home and had not failed to express her feelings about him.

Lathika said, 'How do we formally meet his parents for discussing all this? We must find out more about his family and their likes and dislikes. Your father has met Anil's parents briefly.'

'I can provide you their telephone numbers or ask Anil to tell his parents to contact you.' Parvathi didn't know how the matter should proceed further.

'Give me the telephone number. I shall contact them from my office soon.' Nair said as he got up to be ready for office. Lathika wrote the telephone numbers on a piece of paper and passed it to her father.

Nair realized that his daughter remembered the phone numbers by heart and didn't need to look up anywhere.

At half past ten Nair called Chawla's home and Lovely picked up the phone. Nair introduced himself as Parvathi's father and asked for Sunil Chawla who immediately came on line. After exchanging pleasantries, Nair expressed his desire to meet them at their convenience. Chawla told Nair that he and Ritu were also looking forward to meet him and

Mrs. Nair and invited them to have dinner next Friday at Hotel Taj Mansingh.

Nair agreed.

***

NINETEEN

Nair told Lathika and Parvathi that the dinner meeting with Mr. Chawla and his wife had been fixed for Friday. He told them about House of Ming, the Chinese restaurant in Taj Hotel on Mansingh Road as the venue.

'It's good. I don't like Punjabi and Mughlai cuisine. The Hotel can't serve good Kerala food, so Chinese is fine. It's so nice Mr. Chawla is not forcing us to eat Punjabi food.'

'Mom, for a formal dinner meeting, why do you have to be so fussy about cuisine? The basic purpose is to meet them, not the dinner, isn't it?'

'Yes, but bad food spoils the mood,' Lathika answered.

'I have different view on this. One should meet with an open mind and not with preconceived notions about food, place of meeting or the time. A mind is like a parachute, it works best when open.' Parvathi was smiling.

Lathika didn't like her daughter advising her to meet them with an open or closed mind. She believed that the present generation no longer understood the importance of the saying 'a stitch in time saves nine'. She was convinced that in matrimonial matters, from horoscope matching to looking into family history, everything had its own importance and remembered her own marriage and how her parents had taken care to find out about Nair and his family. Lathika considered it a difficult task these days. She had heard so many marriages going the wrong way and did not want to take chances. She believed that children at present did not understand how sensitive it was for the parents to look for a suitable groom and if parents probed and evaluated the other family, they were considered orthodox and prying in nature.

'I have an open mind Parvathi. That's why I am meeting them,' Lathika quipped.

'Then do remember Mom that they are Punjabis and we are Malayali. They are fond of their food as we are fond of ours. They are from business class where as we are salaried people. We both have to learn, tolerate and appreciate the differences between the two communities otherwise there is no point in taking the issue further.' Parvathi tried to brief her parents.

Nair didn't appreciate his daughter telling them about the basics. But he chose to keep his feelings to himself.

'I think Parvathi is right. Once we have decided to meet Chawla, we should go there to learn about them and make them understand us better. We should not meet with pre-conceived notions about anything.' Nair looked at Lathika who had not enjoyed this briefing from her daughter. He asked Parvathi, 'Since you know Anil better and have met Chawla and his wife, could you tell us more about them?'

Parvathi told her parents about Chawla's background, how they migrated from Pakistan, started from scratch, built up their own business and married within their own community of Punjabis. No one in the Chawla family had married outside their community. She told her parents about Ritu Chawla and her fondness for socializing and partying with her friends. She informed her parents about Ritu's penchant for fashion shows. Parvathi briefed them how Ritu had raised her sons who are doing well and only when she was free from her responsibilities she started clubbing and socializing.

Parvathi added, 'They are not highly educated as their early life was more or less used in building up business from a scratch. Chawla may not have completed graduation. To cover up their inadequacy at times money comes handy and a flashy style is adopted to provide psychological satisfaction. But on the whole they are sincere, family oriented, worldly wise and genuine people. One needs to go a bit deep to understand them.'

Lathika thought her daughter had really gone quite deep into all this. She wondered whether Parvathi knew about Anil's family more than Anil. She mentally repeated her daughters words- sincere, family oriented, worldly wise and genuine- and pondered if any adjective was left. Nair and Lathika exchanged meaningful glances.

'We would try to remember all this when we meet them,' Lathika sarcastically said.

'And Mom, you have to be your natural self. There is no need to present yourself what you are not. They would like your fondness for your culture and traditions as much as they like their own. I have never heard Anil or his parents running down any other community.' Parvathi continued.

Lathika and Nair wondered if ever they showed off or ran down someone.

'Parvathi, how come you know this so well? And do you have to really tell us all this as if we don't know how to present ourselves?' Nair asked.

Parvathi realized she had told her parents far more than required and they would now suspect of something between Anil and her.

'Not at all, I was just reiterating and highlighting the differences between our two families. I have met Anil's family thrice and I thought I should share my impressions. That's all. I am sorry if I sounded like teaching you both,' Parvathi said, realizing her eagerness had made her choose wrong words.

'That's fine *beta*. Let's see how it goes. I hope the Chawla family is liberal in outlook.' Nair wasn't very much sure about Chawla and his wife. He knew by experience that matrimony is different than socializing.

Parvathi thought she may not get a second chance to air her views and remembering Anil's words tried to brief them further. 'Both families may not like each other's food, customs or traditions in its entirety but certainly there are areas and points of convergence. They may like south Indian *Dosa*, *Idlis*, *Sambhar*, *Uthappam* or fish curry but they don't have to like everything we eat. Similarly we may like part of their traditions, culture and cuisine not the whole. I know Anil had enjoyed festivities in Kerala as much as his own 'Bhangra' dance and Baisakhi.'

'We have no problem with their culture Parvathi. We have lived here long enough to know the differences between north and south. But they don't matter to us as long as they don't matter to you. So don't feel concerned about this,' Nair explained calmly.

Lathika agreeing with her husband told Parvathi that as parents it was their duty to find out about Anil and his family and make their own judgment. She told her that as parents they would like to fulfill their obligations, whether someone liked it or not.

They talked about Chawla's family size, business, house and Parvathi felt confident that she was able to clear some of the haze surrounding Ritu and Sunil Chawla. Luckily, no one talked about the recent incident in the family of Ramesh Chawla as she had convinced them earlier that it was an individual act of a desperate person and had nothing to do with either Ritu or Sunil Chawla and his immediate family. Moreover, nothing further had been heard about the incident and according to what Anil told her, Ramesh and his wife had accepted Madhvan.

****

At night when Lathika and Nair retired to the confines of their bedroom Lathika voiced her concern again about her daughter's preference for a north Indian family. Though she had liked Anil yet her mind was not completely at ease. As the dinner meeting with Chawla was coming near, Lathika needed her doubts about the entire match making exercise to be removed.

She asked Nair, 'Are you sure we are doing the right thing?'

'What do you mean?'

'I mean do we really have to agree to what Parvathi has proposed? Do you think marriage between a south Indian and north Indian will work in the long run?' Lathika showed her concerns.

'Why not, marriages are about commitment from both sides. Love marriages and arranged marriages have equal chance of working out. Let's not feel shy about opting for any of the two. We have looked for a Keralite match but failed. We like the boy Anil. It only remains to be seen how Mr and Mrs. Chawla view the entire thing.' Nair was serious.

'At times I feel worried about Parvathi.' Lathika persisted.

'See, to have the guts and to stand up for your beliefs and marry the person you fancy, despite daunting odds, is a challenge. There is no better reason to give up your independence than to be with a person you love and who loves you. I agree that love alone is no guarantee, at the end of the day it's back to commitment.' Nair explained as if teaching a group of young students.

'But marriage into a north Indian family has its own complications.'

'Love is meant to overcome all odds and embrace any and every complication. If one opts for a love marriage or is guided by the compatibility issue then one should assume full responsibility for the decision. One should be prepared to take whatever comes with the terrain. I feel our Parvathi likes Anil as much as he likes her. Let them be happy with it.' Nair tried to remove Lathika's concerns.

Lathika remained silent.

'See we met in Kochi years ago. Our marriage has worked out well. I know arranged marriages within communities have worked for centuries in India and love marriages are only fifty years old. And both can fail. Let's sail with the flow of the current.' Nair made it final.

Lathika thought she had no option but to agree with her husband and daughter.

****

As Parvathi opened her mailbox on internet she found an anonymous mail from someone who signed as 'well-wisher'. Mentioning about the recent events in Chawla family, the mail was meant to caution Parvathi about Anil and his Punjabi family. It said that Chawla family hated south Indians and would never consent for their son's marriage with a south Indian. It hinted about various flings Anil had with females in office, especially Sheila.

Parvathi thought about it for a moment and took it as an act of a jealous colleague trying to poison her mind. Since the facts mentioned in the mail were in the public domain, they didn't interest Parvathi. Anil had told her about her cousin's affair with a south Indian man Madhvan and their marriage. He had been critical of his uncle's stupid attempt to break that marriage and resorting to violence.

But what took Parvathi by surprise was the mention of the dates in the mail about his Goa trip with Sheila. The cottage number in the Hotel Taj Village was also provided. Anil had told her casually about his various trips in India and abroad including Goa but staying with Sheila in the same cottage was entirely different. It disturbed her and her curiosity drove her to call the hotel and check it for herself. Hotel Taj Village had been hosting conferences for Global Logix for last many years and it took them only few minutes to check their computers and inform Parvathi that the cottage was booked in the name of Anil and he was the sole occupant.

Despite the fact that Parvathi heaved a sigh of relief and sent the mail to trash, a seed of distrust was planted in her mind which could either grow through future actions of Anil or wither away by lack of nurture.

****

'I hope Ramesh's stupid act does not affect the mindset of Mr and Mrs. Nair.' Chawla Bhai, addressing no one in particular at the breakfast table, said.'

'Oh, don't bother. I don't think an individual stupid act would be considered typical of any family or community Papa,' Anil said. 'Mr. Nair is an educated person serving as a senior officer for last thirty years. Mrs. Nair taught in college and is well informed,' he added.

Chawla mentioned about the dinner meeting fixed for Friday evening at the House of Ming in Taj on Mansingh Road.

Ritu asked Anil, 'Beta, tell me something about Parvathi's mother. I can't stand south Indians who are rigid and dislike everything from North. I had a few members in my club who considered themselves intellectually superior and ridiculed our Punjabi way of life, calling it loud and brash. How is she like?'

'Mom, I don't know her that closely and have met her twice. Based on whatever I have heard through Parvathi, her mother is a simple, educated lady deeply rooted in her culture. She is not the type who would run down others or mock at different cultural traditions. She likes her cuisine, festivals and dresses as we do. Mr Nair is a practical person who has served here for thirty years and knows about Delhi as much as we do. But he is also firmly rooted in his cultural traditions though tolerant of others,' Anil replied.

'I know he takes liquor but does Mr. Nair really like his drinks as much as I do?' Chawla asked in a lighter vein.

'I believe so. Why?' Anil asked a bit perplexed and taking his father seriously.

'Everyone who likes to drink socially is good to talk to. One can connect with them mentally and emotionally.' Chawla Bhai smiled and gave his explanation which others found funny.

As it evoked laughter all around, Ritu remarked, 'Don't drink whiskey more than you can handle. I don't want two drunken persons should be carried away to their cars while I and Mrs. Nair follow them like fools.'

'If both of you join us it would be good foursome. It would only show how quickly we connect mentally and emotionally.' Chawla tried to crack a joke, and added, 'you know few days back scientists revealed that whiskey and beer contain small traces of female hormones. To prove their theory, the scientists fed 50 men 12 pints of beer and 50 men five pegs of whiskey and observed that 100% of them gained weight, talked excessively without making sense, became emotional, and couldn't drive. —No further testing is planned.'

Everyone laughed except Ritu.

'Thanks, keep us out of it. I don't want that you guys should connect to waiters carrying you like leech clinging to its prey.' Ritu's comments evoked further laughter.

At this point Anil thought proper to brief his parents further about do's and don'ts during the dinner meeting. He told Ritu about the family background of Nairs.

'As there is nothing to be compared in financial terms there is hardly any necessity to dwell upon issues concerning properties, cars, business interests or family riches. Mr Nair works for the government and draws a salary. Parvathi's parents know the difference between a salaried person and a successful businessman,' Anil added.

Chawla narrowed his eyes and thought how Anil was teaching him *do's* and *don'ts*. He felt a little odd that they were being told the script in advance and were expected to adhere to it. But as a shrewd father and businessman, he knew when to remain silent.

'I think they would be more interested in knowing about our nature, family life and whether their daughter would be happy in our family or not. Papa, you don't have to talk in English. They know Hindi, so don't feel constrained,' Anil suggested. 'I don't have to advise you about that as you know everything,' he hastened to add.

Ritu and Chawla wondered whether this wedding was really their first in the family. They could sense with amusement Anil's eagerness for this particular matrimonial match and marveled at Anil's efforts to groom them for the dinner meeting with Nair and his wife. Ritu and Chawla were amazed at their son's efforts to prepare them for the meeting as if he was the only one who was concerned about this match making.

Ritu asked, a bit irritated at too much discussion about dinner meeting, 'What should I and your Papa wear for the occasion? Can I talk in English or I have to learn Malayali?'

'Wear whatever you both feel comfortable in...... Why should you learn Malayali? Talk the way you want to,' Anil fumbled for words failing to catch the sarcasm.

'I'll wear a lounge suit and you can wear a saree instead of shirt and trousers. After all we are going to meet Nairs because of Anil.' Chawla advised with his tongue in cheek.

'I never wear trousers and shirt for formal dinner. I always wear saree,' Ritu snapped.

Chawla thought, 'My wife has the last word in any argument. Anything he says after that is the beginning of a new argument.'

'So Anil is there anything else you would like us to do there or want to advise us about Nair family?' Chawla a bit peeved, probed further.

Anil desperately wanted to tell them to fix the wedding there and then in the dinner meeting at Taj but said, 'Nothing that I can think of at the moment. I shouldn't be advising you as you know a lot more than me.'

'Thanks for your advice beta.' Chawla exchanged glance with Ritu who understood him. They felt happy knowing their son Anil was eager for the alliance and without feeling bad about his attempt to groom them for the dinner; they would try their best as they liked Parvathi.

****

Lathika and Nair alighted from their car in the covered portico of the hotel at five minutes to eight. Nair was dressed in a suit and Lathika wore a silk saree with jasmine flowers in her hair. The impressive looking guard in a white uniform with brass buttons and colorful turban on his head saluted them and opened the glass door. They stepped into the lavishly decorated hall with a marble floor full of intricate designs. Men and women dressed elegantly sat on sofas and talked in low voices. They saw a massive chandelier hung from the ceiling as soft music was played from invisible instrument. They stood looking at the artificial pool containing flowers, asked a hostess for the Chinese restaurant House of Ming and were escorted to its door.

The restaurant was bustling with customers. They noticed brass lanterns hung from the ceiling made of wood. The interior walls were adorned with golden dragons. The furniture looked elegant. The waitress, a chinky-eyed girl in a long slinky dress came to them and Nair asked for Mr and Mrs. Chawla. The waitress directed them to the table where Chawla and Ritu were seated from before and busy talking. On seeing Nair and a lady walk towards their table they immediately recognized their guests and Chawla shook Nair's hands and introduced himself and Ritu to Nair and Lathika. Lathika folded her hands in Namastey. Nair and his wife sat down opposite them.

The waitress arrived and poured water in the glasses and placed the menu in front of each of the four guests.

'What would you like?' Ritu asked Lathika.

'Whatever you like *ji*. You must have come here many times. Whatever is good I can have the same.'

Chawla asked Nair, 'what would you prefer for drink?'

'Whiskey with soda and ice is '*wogay*' for me.' Nair said.

Chawla wondered what '*wogay*' means, then realized Malayali use it to say O.K.

'What about you Mrs. Nair?' Ritu asked.

'A glass of *jaljeera* is fine.' Lathika said looking from the drinks menu.

The waitress arrived again and took the orders and went. Nair said, 'We are so happy to meet you and your beautiful wife Chawla*ji*. Our children work together in the same Company. I have met your son before, once during Onam party in September and later when he came home for dinner. He is a very intelligent and well qualified. My daughter told me she met both Chawla *Ungleji* and Ritu *Aandyji* at the fashion show and later when Ritu *Aandyji* invited her for lunch. She has been showering praises on you both, especially Ritu*ji* who she calls her ideal.'

Ritu did not take long to understand that Aandy*ji* refers to middle aged female in Kerala. The opening remarks of Nair floored Ritu who was extremely pleased to learn that Parvathi considers her as an ideal and has even told her parents.

'She is a very sweet and intelligent girl *Bhai sahib*. I like the way she carries herself and is very well informed about what goes around her.' Ritu was surprised at herself for addressing Nair as *Bhai Sahib* instead of Mr. Nair from the beginning.

'Yes Ritu is right. It's Mrs. Nair who provided her such an environment where she could grow the way she has. Nair *Sahib* must have been busy in his office while *Bhabhiji* must have groomed her daughter,' Chawla said.

'Thank you *ji*, but Mr Nair takes equal interest in our daughter. In fact he was the one who allowed her to go to 'Yemerica' for her higher education. I wanted that she should join her friend Rekha here but she refused. I am happy that you like her. It seems we have done our duty well.' Lathika was pleased with Chawla's sentiments about Parvathi.

They were served drinks. Nair seeing Ritu's glass of lime and soda said, 'Mrs. Chawla you don't have to settle for lime and soda. Why don't you have some wine, unless you don't drink?'

'Thanks. I do take wine but I'll prefer to have lime and soda today,' Ritu said.

Chawla asked, "Is your *jaljeera* '*wogay*'?"

Lathika nodded her head and said, '*wogay*'.

They talked about Anil and Parvathi; their education in 'Yemerica' (America), Chawla's father and his business, Nair's home and family in Kerala.

Ritu realizing that conversation was moving in circles asked Nair, 'Bhai Sahib, our son Anil likes Parvathi and she likes Anil. What do you think about it?'

Before Nair could react Lathika answered, 'Ritu*ji* Anil is a good boy. I must admit that we preferred a Malayali boy for her and advertised on the net but could not find a suitable match. Meanwhile Parvathi introduced us to Anil. We have found him to be very good boy and Parvathi feels comfortable and compatible with him. We are not very rich but have given the right upbringing to our daughter. Parvathi is touchy and independent by nature. My worries are only about her acceptability in the family. She doesn't know Punjabi language, customs and traditions. As marriage is an institution where families are involved she would learn and evolve with time.'

'Mrs. Nair if the girl wants from inside, she can learn and adapt very fast and for that she has to mentally realign herself with the family of her husband. In case she is guided by her own family and doesn't feel one with her husband's family, it becomes difficult for her to integrate. I have heard marriages go bad these days on account of interference from mothers of girls.' Chawla explained showing his wisdom from experience.

'Chawlaji in our family we believe once a girl goes to another family after marriage, it becomes her family. In her *yaity-six* years (eighty-six years) of life my mother never went back to her parents. I and Lathika are not the types who pry into their daughter's affairs or guide her unnecessarily. Lathika never looked back after marriage. We suffered hardship during our early days in Delhi. I did not have a scooter so traveled by bus to office and back. She never complained about lack of comforts or shared her plight with her own parents. So it depends on family and its sub-culture.' Nair was emotional after drinks.

'Bhai *Saheb* it's really commendable that Parvathi has the necessary background provided by Lathika *Bhabhi* and you. God has given us everything and we don't wish for more except that we get a good daughter in law. Since you have shared your past honestly with us, let me tell you that we are not very much educated ourselves. My father provided me decent education but Chawlaji and our eldest son Amit spent more time in organizing business than looking after their studies. Someone had to build the business from scratch and being eldest Chawla *ji* devoted his entire energy to business and left college. We are simple at heart and like people who are straight and honest. You may call us a bit loud as most of Punjabis are but that's not a big deal as our culture and traditions make us like that. Our folk songs and dances are loud and more physical than subtle.' Ritu became emotional while explaining her views.

Lathika assured Ritu that as far as her fears about interference from others or adaptability of Parvathi to her new surroundings are concerned, they are unfounded and not to be thought about much.

Chawla Bhai and Ritu thought that since Anil and Parvathi like each other and the Nair couple looked simple and straight there was no need to enquire much. In fact, they felt satisfied after talking to Nair and his wife and thought that as they liked Parvathi, nothing else was more important. Parvathi was entering their family and they had no hesitation about that left. Anil would not consent to marry someone else easily so Chawla Bhai and Ritu thought of closing the chapter by announcing their consent for the marriage.

Nair and Lathika thought that they had liked Anil from the beginning and now after meeting with his parents they had no qualms about them. Anil's parents didn't seem snobbish or crass. They pondered over the prospects of finding a match from Kerala and did not see any hope as Parvathi would not consent to marry anyone else.

Chawla Bhai and Nair were not used to thinking deeply after few pegs of liquor. For them alcohol was meant to relax and not to help decide bigger issues of life and matrimony.

Chawla Bhai and Nair had downed their fourth peg of whiskey when they heard Lathika ask Ritu, 'so Rituji, what do you think about Parvathi and Anil?'

Ritu looked at her husband and Chawla who had already made up his mind eagerly interrupted before Ritu could react, 'Bhabhi *ji* let's celebrate now. You and I are to be *Samdhi-samdhin*. You know what it is?' and when Lathika nodded he said, 'as far as we are concerned it's final. We like Parvathi for Anil. What do you say Ritu?'

Ritu already decided, nodded her head in agreement.

Nair shook hands with Chawla and Ritu, and said, 'I could never have thought of getting such a beautiful and understanding.... *samdhin*, more beautiful than our Shakeela or Silk Smitha,' inviting a sharp look from Lathika and quickly added, ' and a Mohan Lal look a like *Samadhi* in *Chawla Saheb*.'

'Who's Mohan Lal? Who are these...Shakeela and Shit what....?' Chawla asked.

'The famous superstars in Malayalam film industry. Shakeela and Silk Smitha have been the reigning queens of Malayalam film Industry.'

Chawla Bhai didn't know whether it was a compliment or a snide remark. Ritu decided to check up her similarities with the two superstars later.

All of a sudden Nair asked, 'Chawla Bhai was there some problem in your brother's family? Lathika's brother is a police officer here and he mentioned something few days back about one Chawla family of Karolbagh attempting to finish off a south Indian old man because his son had eloped with this businessman's daughter and married her. Later through press we came to know that this businessman is your brother. This case really shook our confidence and we were disturbed for a while.'

'You are right. This stupid man happens to be my brother. But not only we live separately we also have separate businesses. No doubt, his act was most demeaning and idiotic. He is a real stupid man,' Chawla explained and added, 'but we have nothing to do with that. You know Nair Sahib, these days there is no dearth of foolish people. He should face the consequences of his act. You should have no misgivings about our family. These press-*wallahs* have also played up the whole thing.'

'I can understand Chawla Bhai. I mentioned this in case you need help of Menon, Lathika's brother, I can request him,' Nair said, forgetting, he had introduced Chawla to Menon and helped Chawla and Omji earlier in a different matter.

'No thanks Nair *Sahib*. I have no concern with his stupid act; the matter is in court now, let the court decide these things.' Chawla thought he would not bite the bait offered by Nair who wanted to know how closely he felt about his brother's case.

They further talked about the marriage customs in Punjabi and Malayali families. Lathika expressed her keenness for certain ceremonies to be held in Kerala and said, 'We will have few ceremonies in Kochi with '*yellifents*' in attendance in a festive atmosphere and also at Delhi according to the customs of Chawla*ji*'s side.

'What's a *yellifent*?' Chawla asked.

'well....a *yellifent* is a *yellifent*, the big animal, father of baby *yellifent*. We have lot of them in Kerala during festive season, all decked up.' Nair lost for words, couldn't explain better.

'Oh, you mean elephant?' Chawla asked and Nair nodded his head vigorously.

Chawla told Nair that he would like to taste '*Toddy*' the local brew in Kerala during the ceremonies and Nair expressed his wish to take part in a '*Bhangra*' dance at next Baisakhi.

Lathika and Ritu knew it was of no use talking to their husbands now as they were high, thought of ending the dinner conversation on a positive note, called for the bill, shook hands, hugged and happily left for their homes.

On their way back the two couples started brooding over how early they could fix the marriage and whether they followed the instructions given by their child or violated them. Both wondered about the worth and the need of such a formal meeting in present times and started reminiscing about their own weddings.

***

TWENTY

Fixing up a wedding in Indian family is the first step towards a long sequence of celebrations. Chawla Bhai and Ritu informed their relatives and friends about Anil's matrimony with Parvathi, first thing in the morning. He had called his two brothers, Omji, Ritu and Lovely's parents previous night itself and announced the news.

Anil had first come to know from Parvathi and was visibly excited and happy. Chawla's brothers, Pramod and Ramesh congratulated him though they didn't seem to be truly excited on hearing the news. So were Lovely and Ritu's parents who doubted Chawla if he was really serious. Om*ji* felt happy and congratulated Chawla Bhai, Ritu and Anil separately. Chawla felt that his relatives and neighbors did not like the idea of Anil marrying into a south Indian family. Moreover their chances of entering into a matrimonial alliance with Chawla family seemed to be over.

'Let us talk to the family priest and fix a date for the ring ceremony,' Ritu said. 'One must choose the best *muhurta*.'

'Sure. We'll have to talk to Nair about the dates. Any Sunday will suit everybody.'

Choices of two auspicious dates were given to Nair and Lathika. Unanimously, it was decided that the ring ceremony shall take place next Sunday at seven in the evening.

Nair and Lathika had informed Chawla that in Kerala the weddings were a simple affair. After consultation with astrologers, auspicious dates were fixed and an engagement ceremony called 'Nischayam' was done at the girl's house where all guests and relatives were informed about the marriage. The bride and the groom didn't have to be present there.

'We should have *raunak shaunak*, *lara lappa* in the engagement party Nair *sahib*.' Chawla had said. On Chawla's insistence they agreed for a hotel ceremony and a celebration.

'Chawlaji, we had cut short 'Pennu Kanal' and 'Veedu Kanal', as there wasn't any need for those ceremonies left,' Lathika said. '*Vivah Nischayam* can be a mix of Nair traditions and Punjabi customs.'

'I have been to Kodaikanal but what are 'Pennu Kanal' and 'Veedu Kanal'?' Asked Chawla.

'They are not places. 'Pennu Kanal' is when the boy and his parents or elders come to visit the girl's house to formally see the girl. It can be a simple affair or a large celebration, where the prospective bride and groom and their families consent to the marriage,' Nair explained. 'The girl's parents also visit the boy's family to know more about him and his family, where their daughter is going to spend the rest of her life. This custom is called 'Veedu Kanal'.'

'Yes, I agree. There is no need for that. We have met each other and also the boy and the girl.' Ritu agreed.

'Our case is entirely different. We know about each other already,' Chawla said.

'What's *Vivah Nischayam*?' Ritu asked.

'Once both the families are satisfied with the alliance, the marriage will be officially announced in the presence of the elders and close friends, which is called *Vivah Nischayam*.

It may be a simple affair or a large celebration, depending on our wish and convenience. In some families, the wedding rings are exchanged during this function, and in some other families the exchange of rings are done during the wedding ceremony. We can have a ring ceremony as it goes with your customs as well,' Nair replied.

It no longer remained a small ceremony where only close relatives and friends from both sides were to be invited. A hall which could accommodate more than two hundred people was booked at Hotel Taj Palace in New Delhi. The ceremony was to be followed by cocktails and dinner. Chawla and Ritu's friends had to add to the *raunak shaunak* at the Taj so elaborate arrangements were planned.

On the engagement day or '*Vivah Nischayam*' around three hundred and fifty guests assembled at the Taj Palace hotel. Omji received them at the door. The hall was jam packed.

Parvathi dressed in a red 'Kanjeevaram' silk saree, jasmine flowers in her hair and heavy gold jewelry, looked stunning. Her saree, with its rich and luscious hues and the artistic design of the border and the *pallu* stood apart from the rest. The *zari* work in the border, woven in gold and silver stood out in the artificial focused lights in the ceremonial hall of the hotel.

Anil was dressed in cream silk *Jodhpur* suit and brown shoes. Chawla Bhai and Nair wore lounge suits and Ritu and Lathika were draped in heavy sarees.

Parvathi asked Anil, 'how do I look?'

'Just like a Christmas tree. Only Santa is missing.' Anil whispered back and thought he was being clever.

'Your beer belly makes you look like Santa.' Parvathi's retort was sharp.

He understood. Parvathi was no longer a colleague or a friend. She was the fiancée.

The festivities took only half an hour. Rings were exchanged and cocktails followed. The DJ played groovy music and young and old danced and gyrated to the tune. As the evening progressed requests for Punjabi songs came from many guests and 'Bhangra' beats reverberated.

Anil's friends pushed Anil and Parvathi to the dance floor and surrounded them dancing to the beats of Punjabi songs. Anil and Parvathi also danced with their friends and relatives.

Liquor flowed like water and Chawla Bhai, Om*ji* and Nair enjoyed their whiskey. Senior colleagues from Nair's office had come to the get together and appreciated Anil and Parvathi as a pair and complimented Ritu-Chawla Bhai and Nair-Lathika. Chawla Bhai and his family danced while Nair placed himself in a corner.

When Ramaswamy, the Secretary of Health, Government of India and Nair's boss asked him why he wasn't on the floor, Nair replied, 'Sir, get a few north Indians together in a celebratory mood and inevitably they will switch to the lowest common denominator, which is 'Bhangra'. I like doing it and have done a bit but how long can I keep my hands up in the air as if I'm trying to finger God in his heaven or change a light bulb, I say?'

Guests started to have dinner as the young continued with their dance. The engagement party lasted long and was over only after midnight, late according to Nair, who already felt sleepy.

Being a grand engagement party it soon became the talk of the town. Ritu and Chawla Bhai received congratulatory messages for weeks after the party. Ritu had invited few journalists to cover the ceremony for page three in the city supplements of newspapers. She looked regal in her attire and so were Anil and Parvathi. Chawla Bhai and Nair carried their drink glasses to the readers.

****

Anil and Parvathi knew the news about their engagement would travel like a wild fire in their office. Soon they found themselves hosting another small party for the office colleagues who had missed the event.

But Chawla and Nair had other things to do. After fixing the date for the wedding in March, a month ahead, they got busy with the preparations.

Ritu and Lathika started spending more time in the market, buying ornaments, clothes and other necessities for the wedding.

Anil got busy with his work as he had decided to take one month leave for the wedding. He had planned to stop for few days in Kerala, on Parvathi's insistence, on way to South Africa for their honeymoon. For that he needed to finish his pending projects on a war footing.

Completing pending projects meant less time with Parvathi and absolutely no late outings with her. Only on Saturdays and Sundays they could manage to be together. He, being a supervisor, spent more time in his plush office than before and when Parvathi dropped by in his office before leaving everyday, she found him deeply engrossed with his team members. Anil's group members were quite considerate and moved to another room when Parvathi dropped in to allow the newly engaged privacy to kiss each other bye. Anil and Parvathi relied more on SMS to keep in touch.

At times Parvathi felt slight exasperation about Anil not responding to her calls. But being an understanding and reasonable fiancée, she never showed her growing frustration.

Anil too, made up to her by sharing with her his progress about the project and assignments.

'It's a matter of few days honey. Then you'll have enough of me,' Anil assured her.

'I can't have enough of you dear. I am very possessive.'

'You know we'll be commuting to office together. Saturdays and Sundays we'll watch movies and dine out. It will be just you and me.' Anil started visualizing the future.

'What about others in the family? I hope you don't want me to ignore them completely and earn a bad name right in the beginning?'

'Of course not, we'll balance our time between us and the family.' Anil assured her. 'But I wish this Project finishes in time. I don't want to reach the marriage hall on a horse back straight from my office.'

Parvathi laughed loudly and asked him if she could be inducted as a team member to assist him in the project.

'No way. You could have been into this right from the start, but we didn't want it ourselves as we preferred our association to remain a secret. And now at this stage when the entire office knows we are engaged, I can't ask the project manager to induct you. Moreover it will take days to brief you and get any output from you,' Anil explained.

'I understand honey. I was just joking.' Parvathi pressed his fingers in an assuring manner.

But her contentment evaporated when one day failing to get replies to her SMS she peeped inside his office room and found Sheila alone with Anil and bent very closely over him, while Anil was sitting and perusing few drawings on the table, his hand resting on her back. Sheila was dressed provocatively in a tight T-shirt and hip hugging jeans and the room smelt of her Channel 5. Her bosom was inches away from Anil's face. Parvathi knocked at the door and entered.

Sheila surprised to see Parvathi enter, moved away from Anil, collected her papers and left, wishing Anil and Parvathi good night with a mysterious smile showing sadistic contentment.

Parvathi boiling inside said, 'this is the reason why you were not responding to my SMS. I know what happens here in this room. Now as we are engaged, perhaps you are back to your old flame.' The seed of distrust planted in her mind earlier found the right moisture to sprout. She remembered the email mentioning about the cottage in the Taj Holiday Village, Goa.

Parvathi walked out as Anil checked his mobile and was surprised to find it on a silent mode. There were two SMSs from Parvathi staring back at him. He followed Parvathi, grabbed her arm and persuaded her to come back to his office and have a word with him in private.

'What's wrong with you Parvathi? Sheila was just showing me the drawings. She is a team member and leaving for Kuwait tomorrow for her presentation.'

'So she has to be all over you to exhibit her drawings? Was she interested in showing her drawings or her figure, standing so close and leaning on you? It's all because you encourage such women that these things happen,' Parvathi said. 'I am going. Don't try to contact me. Enjoy company of such cheap women who fling themselves on you at first opportunity, knowing the other person is engaged and about to marry.'

'Parvathi, you have misunderstood her.'

'Don't take her side. You have purposely inducted her in your team.' Parvathi was indignant. 'And why was your hand resting on her back? Was I dreaming?' She asked.

'No you were not dreaming. I am not taking her side either. I am telling you the truth. I just patted her on the back, congratulating her for the beautiful drawings and power point presentation she had prepared for Kuwait.' Anil was defensive.

'Whatever, this is the second time. Earlier it was in the discotheque where a bitch kissed you in front of my eyes. I am going now. Don't come after me.' Parvathi walked out of the office and drove home. She didn't reply to any of the ten SMS she received from Anil and reached home.

Human brain is highly fertile. Plant a seed and it sprouts and spreads its presence very fast. On way she kept thinking about Anil and Sheila. Parvathi thought that a lustful man can find thousand ways to be with a woman. She imagined them using the cottage in Goa while staying separately. She felt cheated and would have crashed into a motorcycle in the front if she had not applied the brakes all of a sudden.

Rajesh entered Anil's office, as he had seen Anil and Parvathi arguing in the corridor, Anil pleading with her to go back to his office. Now he saw Parvathi rush out and guessed something serious. Anil explained the entire scene to him.

'Don't worry mate, most quarrels amplify a misunderstanding.'

'I am in no mood to listen to your famous quotes Rajesh. Tell me what to do now?'

'Elementary my dear, my own marriage has taught me to believe in the saying that the quarrels of lovers are like summer showers that leave the country more verdant and beautiful. You guys were missing the romance in your life after the engagement. So it was bound to happen, Nature's law. Now go and *patao* her.'

Anil sent an SMS, '*What's more painful? When a person whom you trust, hurts you or the person whom you hurt, still trusts you? Think about that and reply!*'

Still there was no response. Anil left for his home thinking Parvathi's anger would subside soon. When he couldn't talk to her on mobile for next two hours he called her home. He asked Mrs. Nair to put him through to Parvathi as her mobile was not reachable.

Parvathi refused to take the call.

'Anil, Parvathi shall return your call soon. She is talking to her friend on the other line.' Lathika lied.

Lathika asked Parvathi the reasons for her tiff with Anil. Parvathi asked her mother to postpone the wedding as she wanted to make up her mind once again before tying the knot. Lathika was alarmed and mentioned to Nair when he came from office.

'It is said, the quarrels of lovers are the renewal of love. Don't worry, their anger will subside soon.' Nair said dismissing it lightly.

'It's not like this. Anil wanted to talk to her but Parvathi doesn't want to talk to him. I have never seen her in such anger before,' Lathika said, 'She asked me to postpone the wedding. She doesn't tell me the reason also.'

'That's stupid. It's not a child's play, I say. Let me talk to her.' Nair was concerned and irritated.

Nair talked to Parvathi and she told him about what had happened at the discotheque and in the office. Nair could not see Anil's fault anywhere in these two incidents.

'Where is he at fault? If a girl stands close to him how can he avoid that, being engrossed in the papers before him? I know jealousy is a human emotion but it springs from lack of trust or lack of assurance from one's partner.' Nair explained. 'It also comes from a low self image or inferiority complex. If you feel jealous try to learn to act by reason and not be emotion, I say.'

'But Papa, why does he have to encourage such girls?'

Nair was happy Parvathi had listened to what he said.

'See, just because Anil kept his hand on someone's back, does not mean that you are loved any less, or that person is more attractive than you are. Voice out to Anil how you feel so that you can discuss things and he can help you alleviate your jealousy.' Nair reasoned with her. 'Perhaps your fiancée needs more attention and affection than you are giving him. Talk to him and sort it out.'

Parvathi and Lathika kept silent. Parvathi felt her father had a point.

Anil sent another SMS at night. '*I never stopped loving you. I just stopped showing it.*'

At 11 in the night Anil called her mobile which was on silent mode. After few rings, Anil called the home telephone. Parvathi picked the receiver at the same time when Lathika picked its extension.

'I have sent so many messages. Later I called and you never returned my call. Are you still angry at me?' Anil said.

Parvathi's anger had cooled down a bit by now.

'Yes I got all of them. I didn't want to talk to you so didn't reply.'

'I missed you the whole evening.'

'You and missed me? Ha,'

'Yes, if you want to know how much I miss you, try to catch rain drops, The ones you catch is how much you miss me, and the other drops you miss is how much I miss you.'

There was silence on both ends.

'Did you ever share your cottage with this girl Sheila in Goa?' Parvathi asked.

Anil was stunned. He could never imagine Parvathi knowing about their Goa visit. 'Someone may have seen us together in Goa as Sheila could never tell Parvathi. Moreover she didn't stay with him but Rakesh in his cottage. It's also possible that Parvathi may have just heard about this and asking him. Now, she would never believe that Sheila was lusting for Rakesh but would unnecessarily connect her to him. How stupid of him. He should have told Parvathi about their Goa visit and Sheila's presence and her lustful affair with Rakesh.' Anil thought, as his mind raced to find out the source of this information. He was worried she may try to check up with the hotel and the records would tell about her presence and it would only add to Parvathi's suspicions. But he composed himself fast thinking nothing could be done now.

'It's an insinuation Parvathi. Who said this to you? I have never shared my cottage with Sheila or any female ever,' said Anil, feeling indignant.

'No one, I got an anonymous mail long back mentioning the cottage number where you both stayed.' Parvathi was calm.

'Then why don't you check up with the hotel?'

'There is no need for that.' Parvathi's reply was cold.

Anil knew it was Sheila who would have sent the mail to poison Parvathi against him. He knew Parvathi must have checked up with the hotel by now and drawing a blank she's verifying it from him and there was nothing to worry about.

Lathika curious to know about the tiff between the two was listening; she put the phone on speaker mode to make Nair listen to her daughter and Anil. She touched her lips signaling Nair to remain silent.

Anil said, 'remember our association of past six months, honey. How we discussed and made arrangements for the Onam party in September. How you managed the fashion show for Mom. How you got me invited to your home. How we had spent our time, all alone in Kochi? Did you ever feel I didn't love you? Put your hand on your heart and ask yourself.'

Lathika felt she would faint any moment. Nair could not believe his ears.

Anil continued, 'For no fault of mine you are avoiding me. Just remember the good times we had together during last many months to remove any negative feelings inside your mind. It's a question of one month only. We'll be marrying soon.'

'I want to postpone the wedding for some time. I need time to make up my mind.' Parvathi spoke about marriage for the first time after the incident.

'But why? Why do you think wrong about me? During last six months could you find anything in me you disliked? In the discotheque earlier and in office today I have been the victim. I never made any advance towards any girl ever,' Anil said. 'I am suffering because of the acts of these stupid girls.'

'I need time Anil. I'll think over it. We will talk tomorrow as I am tired today and have a headache,' said Parvathi.

'Thanks. We'll talk tomorrow. Take care. Bye.'

'Bye.'

****

Lathika and Nair felt their head spinning and aching after overhearing Anil and Parvathi's conversation. They were stunned and felt cheated by their own daughter and Anil.

Gradually, anger replaced surprise and they thought how the children could take the two families for a ride. 'To start with they kept the affair a secret from both the families and manipulated the families on both sides with subtle finesse. Now when everything is decided and both families satisfied by the choice made, they want to postpone the wedding just because they have quarreled,' Lathika said.

'I think romance loses its charm when it's no longer a secret. After engagement their romance is dead. But I am not going to take it lying down. I won't confront her either but I'll tell Chawla first thing tomorrow about this romance of last few months and how they have manipulated both the families and now want a postponement in order to know the other person better and make up their minds. What rubbish, I say.' Nair was fuming.

'We must tell Chawla and his wife. Like us, they have been fooled by our own children.' Lathika agreed.

'You always thought that people of north can't be trusted. Our daughter is a south Indian and how she and Anil have manipulated us and the north Indian Chawla family.' Nair lamented.

'*Aye aye o*, they were both alone in Kochi. And we didn't know about that. This marriage must take place next month. I shudder to think about that.' Lathika trembling and gesticulating, told her husband.

'What will happen if the wedding is postponed? The wedding cards have gone for print. I have personally invited my seniors and colleagues. Lot of tongues would wag and people would cook up reasons and stories.' Nair felt concerned.

'Worse if the engagement breaks off? We will get a bad name from Kerala to Karol Bagh,' Lathika said

Lathika and Nair talked about their sudden enlightenment for long till they fell to sleep. It was decided that Nair will meet Chawla the following day and tell him everything so that he doesn't agree to any postponement of the wedding.

***

TWENTY-ONE

'Nair speaking, Chawla Bhai how are you?' Nair called early in the morning.

'I am fine Nair *Sahib*. All well? You got up very early today?' Chawla asked wondering why Nair called so early in the morning.

'Yes all well. I want to see you whenever it's convenient to you. It's urgent.'

'Any time, is everything OK?' Chawla worried, asked again.

'Yes, everything is *wogay*. Where do we meet?'

'Why don't you come to Meridian? We can have lunch at two o'clock. Is it fine?'

'*Wogay*. I'll be there. Convey my 'namastey' to Rituji. See you at two o'clock.'

Chawla reached Hotel Meridian at quarter past two and found Nair waiting for him in the Lobby. They both headed to Le Belvedere restaurant for lunch.

Nair briefly narrated the entire conversation between Anil and Parvathi watching the lines on Chawla's face appear and disappear fast. He told Chawla that Anil and Parvathi knew each other for last six months, dating each other and had been to Kochi together.

'I always had this uncanny feeling that my son Anil was dating Parvathi and both like each other,' Chawla said. 'But

I wonder how can they have second thoughts about the marriage or consider a postponement.'

'Chawla Bhai we'll be the laughing stock. We must do something. I am sure there is no problem from Anil's side. I shared with you because you should know the facts in case Anil requests for a postponement under pressure from my daughter. Just don't agree to it,' Nair said. 'We are not against this marriage but we don't want to be fooled anymore.' He hastened to add.

'Of course I can't agree. They can't experiment on us like this. But let us give them few days to sort out their misunderstanding.' Chawla was lost in thought.

'Sure,' Nair said while leaving the hotel for his office.

Chawla shared the information with Ritu and told her not to mention it to Anil. She agreed.

****

Anil sent Parvathi a SMS in the morning, '*The minute you think of giving up any relation, think of the reason why you held it so long. Good morning and have a nice day.*'

In reply he got a SMS of thanks and wishing him good morning.

In office Anil tried to contact Parvathi, but she avoided him sounding very busy. He kept on trying her internal number but she did not agree to talk to him face to face.

"Anil, I need some time to think. Why don't you call Sheila for company in case you feel bored?' She said sarcastically.

"I don't have to. We need to talk alone.' Anil pleaded, 'Just hear me out and decide for yourself.'

'I will, only when I am mentally and emotionally ready. Don't press me like this.'

'OK, as you wish.' Anil hung up, disappointed.

****

When everyone was assembled for dinner, Chawla mentioned that the wedding cards have been printed and soon the distribution would commence.

'Can't we postpone the wedding for few days?' Anil asked his father.

'Why? Is there any problem?' Chawla asked, sounding ignorant.

'None from my side,' Anil hastened to reply. 'Parvathi wants a postponement as she needs time to think about this marriage.'

'What do you have to think now? You both are engaged and about to marry.'

'Don't know for sure. She wants to talk to me about our marriage. She is not fully sure about me perhaps,' Anil cautiously said.

'What does it mean?' Ritu asked.

'She feels I am not committed to her. She saw me alone with a female colleague and lost her temper. I have to explain my position to her,' Anil admitted sullenly.

Ritu couldn't hide her annoyance over this.

'Are you both crazy? You knew each other and were friends and then got engaged openly involving relatives and friends and now you have to find out your mutual commitments? Is this a problem with your generation or very specific to both of you? Ritu flared, 'are we a bunch of stupid people who can be driven around according to the whims and fancies of two US educated mature professionals?'

'Mom… there is no confusion from my side. Parvathi… needs to talk…. to me and… be sure about me.' Anil stammered.

'This is not a child's game Anil. Let me talk to Parvathi and sort it out for both of you.' Ritu started dialing Parvathi's mobile.

'Parvathi beta, I need to talk to you. Can you come over? I am sending the car.'

'Ye…s auntie,' Parvathi speechless for a second, sensed something was wrong and managed to reply. 'I'll come over.'

'Thanks, I am waiting for you.' Parvathi hung up.

Parvathi reached Chawla's residence before ten in the night and soon the whole Chawla family gathered around her in expectation. When Parvathi was on way, Chawla Bhai had earlier requested Nair and Lathika to join a bit late and without informing Parvathi beforehand.

Parvathi, without mincing words, told Ritu and Chawla Bhai her misgivings about Anil. She admitted to her experiencing a clash between her head and heart. On account of uncertainty in her mind she wanted to wait not that she didn't trust Anil or was having second thoughts about the marriage. Parvathi confessed that since her own family wanted her to marry a Malayali boy from Kerala, now she felt shaken by the two incidents, though insignificant in nature. She wanted to be very sure before taking the plunge.

'I appreciate Anil's point of view as well that he could not be blamed for the stupid acts of those girls,' Parvathi said. 'But I don't want to be proved wrong in the eyes of my parents.'

She started sobbing.

Ritu draped her hand around her as Chawla Bhai said, 'Beta the earlier incident in discotheque was way back in the past and you got over it well. After that you both have been together and went for engagement with full understanding. So don't bring up the past again. About the present incident I can say that if you both open a quarrel linking past and present, you'll find that you have lost the future.'

'Let me say something. When you first met, may be the similarities you found with each other instantly created the bond and rapport. As you knew each other better, it were your differences that potentially fashioned the strength of your relationship. Therefore you both should value the differences that made you unique as a couple. There might have been times when you wanted to change Anil into your view of his potential. But even if you'd succeeded in your crusade, chances were you'd have lost respect for him for allowing you to have done it and for not having the personal strength to be his own self. So its better that you both learn to compromise and meet halfway every time a conflict surged. Instead of seeing yourself as two separate individuals practice seeing each other as an aspect of yourselves.' Ritu made an attempt to explain.

Parvathi nodded silently. Nair and Lathika also joined in. Parvathi and Anil were surprised to see them there. They settled down with Chawla grim faced, not wanting to interrupt Ritu.

'When expectations are not met, a spat usually ushers in,' Ritu addressing Anil and Parvathi said. 'Determine which expectations are most important to you and which are most important to your partner. Spend some time tossing around what you both desire and need from the relationship and what you must have and won't tolerate from each other. Remember, love work best when it involves both give and take.'

Everyone remained silent in anticipation of further summons from Ritu.

'If educated persons like you both seem one minute like lovesick turtle doves teasing, laughing and giggling with all your might, then few minutes later you begin yelling and berating each other kicking off a lover's quarrel it is unfortunate. A little bantering is what it takes to stoke up a rising emotional tension,' Ritu exhorted them. She asked, 'We have been married for more than twenty five years now and I am speaking from my own experience, tell me had this incident in office occurred after marriage what would you have done Parvathi?'

Anil and Parvathi remained silent with their heads down like two children being scolded in a class room. Parvathi had realized by now that she had overreacted and linked the discotheque incident with Sheila presence in Anil's office. She recognized that had she not received the anonymous email, her reaction towards the occurrence would have been different. Now since the contents of the email turned out to be false, she should forget her misplaced concerns.

'I am sorry Auntie.' Parvathi broke the silence and faces all around her lit up.

Ritu cupped Parvathi's face in her hands and kissed her forehead. Anil smiled after long.

Chawla, Nair and Lathika complimented Ritu for her exposition and making Parvathi and Anil realize the reasons for their spat. Chawla felt like celebrating the moment and offered French red wine to Nair who readily accepted.

When Amit and Lovely led Anil and Parvathi to another room, Nair already tasting wine said, 'I have read that the trouble with some women is that they get excited about nothing- and then marry him'

Chawla agreed and added, 'never trust a fiancée too far or a bachelor too near.'

Ritu said, 'men owe their success to their wives.'

Chawla retorted, 'men also owe their wives to their success.'

'Now don't start a quarrel here, Chawla Bhai,' Lathika said.

It made everyone laugh.

Anil and Parvathi remorsefully looking into each other's eyes shook hands and hugged each other in the adjoining room as Amit and Lovely watched with amusement.

***

TWENTY-TWO

The spat over, preparations for the wedding turned into full swing. Lathika and Nair fixed the date for a traditional feast at their home. It was planned to be a day before the actual wedding with a five course vegetarian meal. A farm house on Mehrauli road was chosen as the venue for the wedding. Nair in Malayali traditions had earlier suggested Parvathi's maternal uncle Menon's home for wedding but it was considered small for the huge gathering expected, so the convenience of a farm house turned out to be the choice of the majority in both the families by a large margin.

As simplicity and brevity mark a typical Malayali Nair wedding, Lathika and Nair did not like to arrange for elaborate arrangements and decoration. But on Chawla's insistence they agreed to put up a grand show of lights and flowers.

It was decided that Anil and his wedding procession would start half a kilometer from the gates of the Farm house and reach the wedding venue by nine in the evening as guests were expected to assemble by that time. After a long discussion over the dress to be worn by Anil the two sides agreed that he would wear a '*sherwani*' and '*chooridar pyjama*' with the decorated customary turban. Anil refused to entertain any thought of wearing a dhoti and an 'angvastram' which Lathika had suggested.

Ritu and Chawla Bhai apprised Nair's about their custom of 'seven pheras' and chanting of 'mantras' by the family priest. Lathika told them about their custom called 'veli' or three circles or 'pheras' around *agni* (fire). It was finally agreed that there would be a proper mix of the customs from both sides. Nair would perform the ritual of giving the bride's hand to the groom, the 'kanyadaanam' or *penkoda*. Nair and Lathika insisted upon a short ceremony of 'sparsham'. A vegetarian meal would follow. Chawla and Ritu readily agreed.

It was decided that all ceremonies would be performed in Delhi as visiting Kerala to perform any ceremony was not found practical and feasible.

With the rough outline of the wedding agreed upon, both Nair's and Chawla's involved themselves in day to day preparations of the wedding.

Parvathi and Anil helped each other in selection of dresses and finally booked their honeymoon destination, South Africa following a short visit to Kerala.

****

On wedding day Parvathi wore a traditional two piece saree adorned with flowers and heavy jewellery and looked very pretty. The marriage procession started half an hour late and Anil dressed in a white '*sherwani*' with matching '*chooridar pyjama*' and cream colored turban, looked royal and handsome. All males wore pink turbans and a scarf round their neck.

It was a grand wedding procession and it seemed the entire Delhi had come to attend the ceremony. Friends and relatives stopped the procession every five minutes and danced to the band and drum beats. Liquor flowed freely as a van was converted into a mobile bar and most of the males in the procession quickly gulped beer, wine and whiskey. It took more than half an hour of walking and dancing to cover a distance of five hundred meters to the venue of the wedding. Hundreds of currency notes were distributed to the band players at each stoppage for dance.

Nair, his family and friends welcomed the procession at the door and helped Anil get off the horse and walk up to the stage and wait for his bride. Parvathi entered demurely with a garland in her hand. Anil put the garland round her neck and when Parvathi tried doing it, Anil's friends already tipsy, lifted him high to make her reach Anil's neck difficult. The exchange of garlands was followed by guests wishing Anil and Parvathi a happy married life and photographs were taken.

As guests headed for the makeshift bar, the groom, his parents and few other relatives and guests assembled in the covered hall where Nair asked Anil to take off shoes and washed his feet. The actual 'Phera' ceremony started according to the auspicious time fixed by the family priests. After three rounds around the wedding fire were taken Nair stopped Anil and Parvathi. Anil and Chawla were perplexed but Nair tied a 'Taali' strung on a yellow thread around the neck of the bride. After this ceremonial ritual remaining four 'pheras' were taken. Nair performed the ritual of giving Parvathi's hand to the groom, the 'kanyadaanam' or 'penkoda' after all the seven 'pheras' were performed.

'This handshake shouldn't be a formality just like two boxers shaking hands before the fight begins,' Rajesh, Anil's friend said. Everyone laughed and Anil and Parvathi remembered their own spat few weeks before.

Lathika insisted upon a short ceremony of 'sparsham' and made Anil sit in front of the bride, tilt his head backwards to touch the bride's forehead as Parvathi offered puffed rice or *laja* to the fire. As the chanting of mantras started, Anil was asked to lift the bride's foot and place it on the *Ammi* or the grinding stone. He hesitated and looked at Ritu who was smiling. Nair announced that this step signifies the breaking of ties from her old family.

'But why should she break ties from her old family?' asked Anil.

'It's a custom Anil. We must follow it,' Lathika replied as everyone watched quite amused.

Late Anil was asked to move Parvathi's foot forward seven times with his hand symbolizing her entry into his family. Anil thought about it and looked at his father who shrugged his shoulders and decided resistance to the custom was useless and moved her foot as Parvathi giggled.

After the nuptial rites over, it was time for dinner.

Chawla asked Nair, 'Let's both of us have 'pheras' with our Ritu and Lathika.'

Ritu hearing him interrupted, 'Forget it. Once is enough. I am paying its price till today. I can have reverse 'pheras' if you want.'

Nair couldn't follow and asked its meaning. Chawla said 'certain things are better not explained, Nair *Sahib*.'

After midnight Anil and his parents left with Parvathi for their home leaving Nair and Lathika weeping. Certain rituals were observed on reaching Chawla's house.

Anil and Parvathi took the flight to Kochi the following evening on way to South Africa.

****

Anil and Parvathi checked into the same hotel where they stayed on their last visit. But this time their stay was entirely different. They didn't feel like coming out of their suite till they had to catch their next flight to Mumbai for their South African journey.

'It's a mission accomplished. Isn't it?' Anil looked at Parvathi's glowing face.

'Yes my dear husband. We never worked so hard on any project as this one. After all it's a success.'

'Yes it is,' Anil replied and took Parvathi again in his arms.

In the morning they came out of the room to check out for the airport. Parvathi and Anil saw Sheila dressed in a skirt and blouse with a newly appointed colleague Khosla enter the hotel lobby. Anil's heart skipped a beat as if he had seen a ghost and looked away. Sheila leaving Khosla behind walked towards them, winked at Anil and wished them good luck as Anil kept his lips sealed, face turned white with horror and looked ninety degrees from Sheila. Anil's heart was pounding as if he had run a marathon. Parvathi glanced at him and seeing his discomfiture couldn't control her laughter. She thanked Sheila and they moved on.

'Why didn't you thank Sheila?'

'I have taken a vow not to see her face ever.'

Parvathi smiled and clutched his hand as Anil gave furtive glances towards his back to ensure Sheila wasn't following him. He wondered when Sheila started this new affair with Khosla and prayed to God it should result in her marriage with him soon.

****

'So, Anil is married now. How do you feel?' Chawla asked.

'It's a great feeling Sunil. Both the sons are well settled,' Ritu replied.

'I wish I had been born in the present time.'

'Why?'

'I could have tried to fool my parents and select a bride of my choice for myself.'

'You stupid, I would have made you select me even then,' Ritu said, her fingers playing with his hair.

'Finally we two are left alone.' Chawla mused.

'Yes. That's true. There will be two daughters in law at home now.'

'What about us?' Chawla asked.

'What about us?'

'Let's go for the second honey-moon to Switzerland this month.' Chawla came closer towards Ritu.

'How is it possible, sir? And what about the Chandigarh fashion event?

'I have heard Rita Beri, Danish Malhotra and Mohit Bal are all going to Switzerland. I thought we might go there as well.' Chawla enticed her.

'Really? How do you know? Let's go there. Book the tickets today. We can request Rekha to postpone the event till we return. After all she is the friend of our own Parvathi.'

'Forget about the Chandigarh show, dear. We will have a real designer fashion show in Switzerland. Remember to keep your bikinis and skirts on our trip to Switzerland. We'll have a private show- just my *titlee* and me,' Chawla said and took Ritu in his arms after months and kissed her.

'Yes you are right.' Ritu enjoying a rare moment like this with Chawla Bhai surrendered herself in his arms and said, 'Forget the Chandigarh show.'